BOOK ONE – THE THEODORIC SAGA

The Crown of Anavrea

By

Rachel Rossano

Also written by Rachel Rossano

The Mercenary's Marriage

Exchange

ISBN 978-1-105-16555-9

The Crown of Anavrea is a work of fiction. Though actual locations may be mentioned, they are used in a fictitious manner and the events and occurrences were invented in the mind and imagination of the author. Similarities of characters to any person, past, present, or future, are coincidental.

Cover by Laura Miller.

Second Printing

This was written for Greg, the man I love, and

Charissa, the best kind of editor,

an enthusiastic one.

The Table of Contents

Chapter I

Eve covered her head and crouched low in the raspberry patch. She concentrated on not making a sound. The blare of the horn and the cries of the hunters faded. Lowering her hands, she strained her ears. Not even the echo of their crashing in the distance remained. The birds stayed silent, but considering the recent ruckus, they might have all fled.

A groan broke the unnatural silence.

She froze and listened, heart in her throat. A pained, male grunt came from about three feet to her left. Cautiously she turned her head. A stranger stared at her through the tangle of bushes between them.

A wild mess of brown hair fell over his dark blue eyes as he regarded her in alarm. Sweat plastered the hair to his forehead. He observed her with more of a feverish glaze than true understanding. Pain etched lines about his eyes.

He opened his mouth as if to speak, but then shook his head. Falling forward, he then rolled onto his back and lay still.

Eve hurried to untangle the thorns from her tunic.

Free at last, she crept out of the patch and approached him. Fear and instinct screamed she should flee. Instead she paused. If she stopped to help him, she would be beaten. Her master warned her to stay away from the king's men.

Well, the king's men or not, the pursuers were gone. As their prey, he could hardly be one of them. Was he worse?

She inched forward and a twig snapped under her knee.

"Go away and leave me be," he ordered.

"What will become of you?"

He stared into the sky above the trees. "My pursuers return." His chest still heaved from his recent exertion. "I die." Restlessly, his hand clenched and released at his side as though he was fighting the urge to run.

"I know of a place where you can hide." She watched his lean form for a reaction. "It is nearby."

He stopped moving. Finally, as though sensing she would not leave, he spoke. "Come over here. I want to see you."

She crept to his side. As soon as she drew close, she could see the source of his pain. A shallow gash ran across his left arm above the elbow and an even more serious injury marred his right leg above the knee. The leggings, torn and caked with a combination of dried and fresh blood, trailed filth in the wound. She was calculating how she could slow the bleeding when he commented.

"You are only a child."

She brought her eyes to his face and bit her tongue. This was not the time to argue her age. She returned to assessing his injuries.

"If you are wondering whether or not I am able to walk, stop."

"I will help." She met his eyes with a cool determination that left no room for doubt.

After a moment, he broke her gaze and returned to staring at the sky.

"What if I want to die?"

She was still thinking about the best reply when she grew aware of his scrutiny. Their eyes met. "Why would you?"

His lips compressed as he swallowed his reply. Instead, he offered, "I understand I do not have a choice."

He resisted as she reached for his wounded arm.

"You need to promise me something first."

She frowned and didn't reply.

"If we are spotted or do not make it into hiding, you must kill me."

She looked away from the pleading and pain in his eyes. "I promise." Her voice was barely audible, but he seemed satisfied. Thankfully he did not ask her to say it again. She concentrated on ripping strips from her chemise. It made her nervous to repeat a promise she didn't intend to keep. *Kurios, don't make me keep the promise,* she prayed.

She bound his leg and arm. After numerous false starts, they managed to gain their feet. He towered over her by a good foot. His injured leg threatened to give out, but otherwise he could easily support himself on his other limb despite the obvious loss of blood. The weight he draped over her shoulders made it clear she wouldn't have been able to budge him on her own.

Conversation was reduced to grunts of pain or effort. Eve began to consider the seriousness of her decision. Mridle wasn't going to allow her to nurse this man. There was no possible way to do it without his knowledge. Escaping her master would be the only way she could care for this man. And if the stranger persisted in his fatalistic outlook, she might not succeed. She shook the thought away. *He must live, Lord. He must live.*

The usual three-minute walk took them forever. Dusk dimmed the sky when they finally reached the broken-down door of the old shed.

The last steps were brutal. A few feet from the door, his good leg gave out. Eve could not carry all his weight. She stumbled under the sudden shift, tripped, and came down painfully on her knees in the mud. Realizing that he might crush her, the man rolled to the side and landed on his back in a small patch of grass. After his stifled cry of anguish, they fell silent. She waited until her knee ceased throbbing before she crawled over to where he lay.

"I will go in and clear a place for you to lie down before we try to move you again."

He nodded his agreement. He had no breath to speak.

She moved as fast as her sore muscles allowed and stumbled inside. A hermit's shack, the one-room structure did not offer much comfort. A fireplace took up most of the right wall. A small cupboard-like lean-to added for storage hid behind a rickety door to the left of the hearth. Leaves and bugs littered the floor and swaths of spider webs rustling with carcasses filled the room. Movement among the clutter and the rotting window coverings did not help her first impression. The only thing resembling a bed crouched along the length of one wall. In essence it was a wooden shelf with an old straw mattress on it. She pulled off the decaying mess and, using her skirt, she brushed off the bugs. Now came the harder part.

Upon returning outside, she almost cried at the sight of him. He managed to prop himself against the wall. In this position, he dozed. Every line of his body screamed discomfort.

Gently, Eve woke him. Together they got him to his feet and through the door. He fell onto the hard pallet. She winced as his face contorted in pain. She knelt near his shoulder to work on making him more comfortable. The gash in his arm needed stitching, which required thread. She glanced at the single window. Twilight veiled the sky and there was much to do.

"What is your name?" His voice wavered so weakly she barely heard him. She met his eyes, dark and glassy with pain and fatigue.

"Eve."

With a shallow, bitter laugh, he said, "How ironic." Then, as if the strength to fight unconsciousness drained from him, his eyes closed, and his head rolled to one side.

For a frantic moment Eve feared she had lost him, but his weak pulse reassured her. She watched his chest rise and fall and tried to decide what to do next.

Darkness crowded out the last light when she finally left him. He still shifted restlessly on the bed, but she could do nothing more without supplies. As a final step before leaving, she removed every weapon on his person. She doubted he would use them, but she wanted to be certain.

First, she returned to the berry thicket. The pail lay where she dropped it. A sheathed knife lay next to a nearby tree, hidden in the grass until her toe found it. Taking these with her, she headed for her master's house. Fear rose up, threatening to override her determination.

"He must have food, warm blankets, and medicine or he will die."

She said the words once aloud, but their essence pushed her forward through her fear. Each step still took great effort. Finally she stood before the aging edifice of her master's house. The sagging roof, broken shutters, and overgrown doorstep offered little assurance of a welcome.

Kurios, give me strength, she prayed before unlatching the back door and entering.

The kitchen glowed with weak light from the banked cooking fire as she slipped through the opening. Her master, Mridle, waited for her with his strap and fist.

"Where were you?" he demanded. "I had to eat supper out."

Eve closed her lips tightly and straightened. She dropped the pail and knife among the boots and then turned to face her

4

punishment.

"Not going to tell me, brat?" Mridle wrapped the whipping strap around his fist. "We shall see about that."

When Mridle purchased her, Eve resolved to never cry in his presence. This time she couldn't hold back the tears. Before he left her, eye swelling shut and blood dripping from her face, Mridle paused.

"You are now the property of Horben."

Horben was the local tavern owner. He kept slave girls for his patrons' entertainment. Eve's golden hair and green eyes had caught his attention years ago.

"He is coming for you tomorrow." Mridle spat at the hearth stone, not even bothering to aim for the slop bucket at his heel. "He will teach you to show respect. Those girls get three choices, obedience, whipping, or worse. Horben is planning a lesson in worse by nightfall, be sure of that." He grinned, showing off his yellow and brown teeth. "He will have you submissive and begging in a few days, mind my words. Then you will wish yourself back here with me."

The moment he was truly gone, clamoring up the stairs to bed, she began getting to her feet. Gingerly working her hip joint where one of his kicks had landed, she glanced around the room with her good eye. She didn't own much, and they would need more. Mentally calculating the value of the government mandated wages due her, she limped around gathering thread, food, bedding, clothing, medicine, and other necessities. Finally, with a bundle on her back and a tinderbox banging her good hip, she left.

Eve realized Mridle might just come after her. Trusting him to make the assumption that she would run as far as possible, she suspected they would be safe for a time in the abandoned hermitage.

When she reached the cabin, Eve stumbled over the doorsill. Fighting the heaviness of her eyes, she tended to the man. His clothes were drenched in sweat and his skin hot to the touch. As she removed the makeshift bandages, she cleaned, stitched, and dressed his wounds. Praying that it would be enough, she covered him with the warmest of the blankets. Each breath hung briefly before their mouths. Now she needed to build a fire.

The previous inhabitant left an abundance of wood behind

5

the building. She cleared out the clutter in the fireplace and built a small blaze. Thankfully the chimney worked, drawing the smoke upwards and outside. After a mild November, the weather was turning. He needed the warmth. After checking on him once more, she allowed herself to lie down between the hearth and the bed.

Eve awoke to a cry of pain and grief. The stranger sat up in the bed, arched in agony as he let out a second guttural yell. She barely intercepted him as he threw himself forward. With all her strength and weight she just managed to get him to return to lying on the wooden slab. He fought her, but the initial lunge apparently exhausted his resources. She did her best to restrain him so he could not hurt himself. He was still quite strong for a sick man.

"You are safe now." She brushed back his hair as he relaxed again. "I am here to help you." He didn't open his eyes, but his face turned into her touch like a small child seeking comfort.

He muttered nonsense as she straightened his blanket. She talked to him as she would a child, describing her actions. Her voice appeared to soothe him. He quieted and relaxed again. Eve got up with a sigh, and then fed and stirred the fire. Twisting her back to stretch the aching muscles, her eyes fell on her charge. His dark eyes scrutinized her, struggling to focus on her face for a few moments before finally sleeping.

For three days, his body fought the infection. He talked, and she listened. He cried out, and she soothed. While she cleaned or moved about, he would lay motionless, gazing at her with distant, glassy eyes. She often wondered if the man she met still existed behind the fits, sweat, and pain. All the while, she prayed.

On the second night, the hallucinations commenced with him yelling in terror for Ireic. It took her an hour of role playing to get him to sleep again. She gathered from his ramblings that Ireic was his brother, but not much else.

Later in the night he called for Atluer and spoke of a Prince Hiaronical. For two hours she attempted to convince him he shouldn't get up and pursue someone named Trina. He became so loud and hysterical she feared discovery. Since their lives were both marked, she fought to quiet him.

Finally he settled again, but not before she grew curious about his past. His memories seemed to focus around his and Atluer's late childhood.

6

The interruptions in the night and long days of hard work took their toll on her own healing body. Early in the third evening, she fell asleep while tending the fire. Her eyes refused to remain open one more minute.

She woke later the same night, and darkness greeted her. The glimmer of embers was gone. Mindfulness of her surroundings slowly awakened and she grew conscious of something soft between her and the floor. When she reached her hands out before her, the fingertips found the rough grain of the shed's outer wall. Realization dawned. She must be lying under the shelf. She rolled over. Her gaze searched out the weak glow in the grate across the room.

She struggled to remember how she ended up there. Then she became aware of his presence, a dark shadow propped against the wall close to her head. By concentrating she detected the shape of his form slumped forward in sleep. Her first thought protested he should not be on the cold floor. Eve crawled over to him.

Worries about his health prodded her. One serious setback and he might never recover. She must move him. Slowly she inched around him. He did not stir at her touch on his arm.

As her questing fingers located his heartbeat at his wrist, he sighed in his sleep and fell forward. She moved to catch him, but he caught himself.

Without a sound, he leaned back again, straightened his legs and adjusted position. His bandaged leg struck the hard wood. Moving away from the obstacle, he bumped his thigh even harder into Eve. This time his eyes flew open in pain. His nose missed her forehead by a breath. He registered her alarm despite the darkness.

"What was that look for?" he asked through gritted teeth. He gingerly guided his leg to a more comfortable position. "Surely you do not think I intend to hurt you?"

She ignored the question. "Let me examine it." She reached to help him. He relaxed against the wood and watched from beneath lowered eyelids as she checked the dressing. She realized she required more light.

Fetching the lamp and lighting it took a good chunk of time because she also needed to coax the fire to life to keep the cold from overwhelming them. The man's eyes followed her, disconcertingly clear and intense. He spoke while she put the burning straw to the wick. "How long since we met?"

Without looking at his face, she returned to his leg and set the light next to it. "Tonight is the end of the third day." She bent to examine the exposed wound as she spoke. Satisfied the stitches had not been damaged; she reassembled the wrapping. He watched her.

"Healing?"

"The infection is leaving slowly," she replied. "It is healing well." She finished the bandaging and for the first time she met his gaze and froze.

Before, pain or fever blocked the way. Now she appreciated their cloudless depth. Nothing muted the force of his scrutiny. Flustered, she tried to continue in her work and treat him like just another patient.

"May I touch your forehead?" She hurried on to explain. "I need to check if you are feverish." Certain her cheeks were red from the warmth flooding them, she was thankful for the dim light.

"Does my arm need examining too?"

Her hands shook as she pushed up his hair and pressed her hand to his forehead.

"Your fever has left." She picked up the lamp. "I will check the shoulder in the morning. You need to get back to the bed. The floor is too cold."

He shifted as she rose, offering her his good arm. "If you pull, I might be able to stand."

"Ready?" she asked, gripping firmly.

He swallowed and then nodded. She pulled and he slowly gained his feet. Slipping an arm around his waist, she bore most of his weight. Together, they crossed the uneven floor to the place he had been laying the evening before. After a series of careful and painful negotiations, the stranger sat on the bed and tried to recover his composure. Pale and drawn, he rested for a moment with his eyes closed. Shivers set in, contorting his arms. She moved to retrieve his blanket from the floor when he reached out and stayed her. She lifted her head and he caught her chin in his hand.

He studied her features. "Thank you."

"You're welcome," she replied in a small shaky voice. His blue eyes were dark and clear. Traces of pain and sadness lingered, still the fever was gone.

Suddenly an expression of concern replaced his smile. His second hand joined his first, framing her face in a gentle, firm grip.

"What is this?" He ran a thumb across her spit bottom lip. "And this?" She guessed he indicated the remainder of a bruised eye. "I was distracted by pain when we met, but I do not remember you appearing so beat up." He frowned. Eve did not know if it was aimed at her or his lack of memory. Either way, something made her tremble.

"Masters have every right to punish their slaves." She stated the fact in a flat voice. Mridle informed her of the law repeatedly as a warning to her. He had exercised these rights often and well on her in the past.

"You are a slave?" The surprise did not detract from the severity in his tone.

"Yes." She paused. "A runaway slave."

With a swiftness that surprised her, he located the leather band around her throat. The circle rested where one had lain for as long as she remembered, above her collarbone pulled snugly against her neck.

"Unbutton your collar so I can see it." Not waiting for her to obey, he searched his pockets for something.

"I removed everything resembling a weapon when we got here."

"Whatever for?" His face hardened with disapproval. She flinched at the intensity of his gaze. He noticed and regret passed behind his eyes. "Sorry. You were correct to do so. I would have done the same. I am sure you were considering my state of mind." She still heard the tension, but she knew she was not the cause.

"I will get them."

"Please do." He moved himself to a more comfortable position. "I want you out of that tonight."

She gathered the items she had hidden: an eating knife, an ornamental blade, and a well-used, wickedly sharp dagger. He chose to use the last one. After instructing her to stand in front of him facing the fire, he started to undo the two buttons she had forgotten.

As he pushed the fabric away from her throat, Eve realized her dangerous position. His knife hung inches from her and she possessed no way of defending herself. Just as she opened her mouth to protest, his hand encircled the thick band and her heartbeat quickened.

With his fingers protecting the skin from bruising, he

slipped the blade into the space between the collar and her slender neck. Carefully he applied pressure to the leather. After only two quick, hard pulls, it gave way.

She did not pay any attention to where it fell because she became preoccupied with her patient. He groaned in pain after the final tug. The clutter moved aside with a sweep of her arm before she urged him to lie down again.

"I should have told you to wait a few days." She shifted the mess to the table.

"I would not have listened."

After a quick check that none of the stitches were torn loose, she replaced the lamp. When she returned to the shelf, she found him waiting for her. Ignoring the man's eyes, she gathered the blanket she used the past few nights and purposefully approached the closet door. As she passed the table, she glanced at him. "Do you need the light?" she asked.

"Where are you going?"

"I will sleep in the lean-to." She forced her voice to be firm. She did not intend to discuss the matter. "Want me to extinguish the lamp?"

A frown indicated he wanted to argue that she not sleep away from the fire, but finally he shook his head. "Yes." He adjusted his position and said, "Good rest," as if dismissing her from his presence.

"Good rest." She blew out the flame. A quick glance behind her verified his eyes were again watching her. After closing the rickety door firmly, she regarded the back wall only inches from her nose.

The space was completely black accept for the star shine seeping through gaps in the boards. Eve tried to concentrate on the woodland around the building rather than the warmer and much larger room beyond. Panic rose in her throat. She forced the fear aside and focused on the sounds of the forest. *Kurios, help me.* Blanket wrapped about her shoulders and huddled against the cold, she settled in for a long restless night.

Bands of light fell across her face. Even as she opened her eyes, she knew she had slept late. Alarm pushed all sleep from her mind. *Mridle is going to beat me again.* She sat up abruptly, striking her skull solidly on the slanted ceiling above her.

"Are you alright?"

The question came from the next room. It made her heart jolt in surprise, and she cracked her head again.

She pushed open the cupboard door and rose as she answered. "Aye."

Her memories from the night before seemed to be more like a dream than reality. To verify they had happened, she put a hand to her throat.

"The collar is on the floor."

Eve jumped at his voice. With forced calmness, she confronted him. He had propped himself up with his good arm and the wall behind him. It was obvious he had been waiting for a while.

Her cheeks grew warm. In an attempt to hide her face, she busied herself at the fire. His gaze made her spine tingle. "Must you always watch me?"

He smiled slowly. "I enjoy watching you."

"I expected you to grow weary of it by now."

Eve moved through the motions of making breakfast. With her hands busy, she hoped that his presence would be easier to deal with.

"What is your name?" she asked.

"I do not want to tell you yet."

"Then what should I call you?" She leaned over to lift the pot to the iron arm above the fire. She had found the thing discarded behind the hut. An hour of hard scrubbing to get rid of the rust and dirt caked inside and it appeared to have years of use left in it.

"You can call me Labren."

He began to move toward the edge of the shelf. Gingerly, he put his legs over the side, healthy one first. His movement caught Eve's attention and she moved to stop him.

"You cannot get up yet." She placed herself in his way.

He looked her in the eye. "I am getting up. Either you assist me or I will do it without help."

"You are not well enough to stand." She put her hands on her hips and placed her feet in a firmer stance. "You will pull out the stitches and slow the healing."

Her position lacked the overbearing air she had hoped for. It was difficult to stare down a man when one had to glare up to meet his eye. Regardless, she stood her ground.

"I was strong enough to move you across the floor last night, and a few hours later, I removed your collar." His eyes filled with a combination of amusement and annoyance. "And I intend to get out of this bed. So, if you refuse to help, will you please move aside?" Although he was amused, he was not asking her this time.

The battle lost, Eve returned to her cooking. Behind her, she heard him land on his feet with a grunt. With the help of the old broom handle, he hobbled outside. As soon as the door closed behind him, she rushed to the window. She glimpsed his broad shoulders as he staggered around the corner of the shack. He had to relieve himself.

Scolding herself for checking on him as if he were a child, she resumed her work. By the time Labren reappeared, the broth was hot and waiting, with some of her dwindling store of bread. Pain and exhaustion pulled at his features as he sat down. The exertion from his short walk increased the pallor of his face.

After filling a bowl with the steaming liquid, she set it in front of him. She moved to return to the fire, but he caught her hand. "Come, sit down. We need to talk." The remaining seat was a three-legged stool. Sitting so much lower than him would make her feel insignificant. She perched on the sleeping ledge across from him instead. For some reason, she did not want to be vulnerable with this man. His large presence intimidated her.

"I know very little about you." He swallowed a spoonful of the thin soup.

"Isn't much to tell."

The expression Labren shot her over his spoon indicated he did not believe her. "I need the details of what happened to you the last time you saw your master." He brought the bowl to his mouth. As he drank, he considered her face over the rim.

She refrained from acknowledging his discreet attention. In a flat tone she related the events as they transpired the evening they had met. "After I left you here, I went to the berry patch. Then, I returned to my owner, Mridle. He was waiting for me. He beat me with his razor strap, and when I didn't cry, he used his fists. I cried."

No shame came with her admission of weakness. Not wanting to dwell on her tears or the next part, she hurried on to finish.

"He threatened me and went to bed. I took the supplies we needed and came here." Labren was silent. Her hands twisted in her lap while she waited for him to speak.

"What did he threaten?" He set his now empty bowl down.

"He said I had been sold to the Tavern owner, Mr. Horben. He keeps girls for the entertainment of his customers. I cannot go there and you needed someone to care for you, so I left." She raised her eyes, but he avoided hers. "Please do not send me back." The plea slipped out unbidden. She bit her tongue.

"Do you have any family?"

She frowned. "A brother, but..." She shook her head.

"A brother?"

"I haven't seen him in years. He is at sea and may even be dead."

Labren sat in silence for a long time. He kept his face hidden in the shadow, cloaking his thoughts from her as well. When he finally spoke, his voice was so tight with control he almost did not get the whole sentence out. "They will not have you."

Another long period of silence followed. In a calmer, but still strained, tone he muttered something. "Any other possible way...." He absentmindedly rotated the bowl in his hands. Eve wondered what he planned, however she was too afraid to ask.

She realized the severity of his injuries three days ago. He would have never given in so quickly when whole. Even now, discomfort still creased lines around his mouth and eyes. She needed a chance to go herb gathering. Maybe a simple herbal tea, the one she used for aches, could ease some of his pain.

"Would you be willing to marry me?" His voice broke into her thoughts and before she processed his question, he continued. "It is the only option I can think of that makes you both unquestionably free and under my protection." Fixing his dark blue eyes on her green ones, he declared. "The problem is...I follow the Kurios and He teaches marriage for life."

Fighting past the instinctive fear that he was going be another form of Horben, she tried to consider the consequences of such a step.

Labren reexamined his motives. He studied her. Strands of warm, honey blonde hair escaped from the braid wound around her crown. They curled about her ears. Pleasing to look at and spirited enough to make life interesting, she appealed to him in many ways. However, the primary appeal was her apparent strength. She presented a brave front. She had survived her master, but no matter how strong her spirit, her body was weak and her position vulnerable. She already sacrificed so much for him; he was responsible for her now.

Her previous master was not an option. Also, their time together in this shack unchaperoned compromised her reputation. In marriage he could keep her close and, hopefully, safe until he finished getting himself out of this mess. The new found intention to build a future for her, for them, filled him with hope. He liked the thought of a future with her.

"What happens if I marry you?"

"After I am well enough to travel, we will go south. I have to get to the capital city. Once there about a month I should be free to earn a living. During that time, we can seek a place for you to stay while I am away."

She stared intensely at her clasped hands.

"What do you expect of me as your wife?"

He frowned.

"Cook our meals. Wash our clothing occasionally. Of course other household chores will need tending." He glanced her way. "Is that what you are asking?"

"Sort of." After a moment or two, she gathered the courage to meet his gaze. "Are you going to want children?"

As he processed the fear in Eve's eyes, visions of his father and brother flashed through his mind. His shoulders hurt from the pressure of an invisible burden. Children were an absolute necessity. How could he tell her when she clearly feared the process? The intensity of the emotion surprised him. It answered his question: did she fear anything?

"Not until you are ready." They had time. She was too young at this point anyway. "How old are you anyway?"

"Twenty-one."

His eyebrows rose. She didn't look it.

"Yes," she took a deep breath, "I will marry you." The fear lingered in her eyes.

He responded without thinking. "Why?"

14

Even though her cheeks flushed a bright red, she met him with a steady gaze. "I want to be free, but I also don't want to starve."

Her words reminded him of another woman. That one had said she would rather starve than marry him. Brushing the painful memory aside, Labren dragged his mind back to the present situation. Eve was not Trina and he no longer lived in the King's palace. He sat at an old table in a falling down hermit's shack near the Northern Mountains. Across from him was not a dark-haired, cold-faced princess. Instead his gaze fell on Eve, a gentle, warm and caring young woman who had just accepted his proposal.

He gave Eve a half smile. "I will try to make you happy you chose me over those options."

She opened her mouth to retort, but instead she bit her lip.

"Where should we go to find a seeker who would be willing to perform such a ceremony?" he asked.

"There is a Servant of the Kurios in the next village. He can help us." Her thoughts were on something else.

"Will he keep your whereabouts a secret?"

"Yes, he is a friend of mine. He tried to buy me from Mridle many times." After a second or two she continued. "You will probably be well enough to travel on foot in a week."

"What about on horseback?"

That got her attention and she focused on him. "In a few days, if necessary. Do you have a horse?"

"No, but I could purchase one and a cart." He smiled to himself at her surprise. "A wagon would be best, don't you think?"

She resumed her thinking. "How will we buy them? Neither one of us should be seen."

"I leave that up to you." Her amazement at his trust crept across her face. "I am sure you know someone who can manage to arrange something."

She was already plotting; thoughts and plans formed behind her eyes. Shakily rising, he limped toward the shelf where she perched on.

"I need to rest. My short walk wore me out."

She moved quickly from her seat. She backed away from him as if he represented something dangerous. After lying down, he contemplated her reactions.

15

Eve returned to her work with an air of preoccupation. He noticed she went out of her way to avoid going near the sleeping ledge, which was quite a challenge in such a small room.

Chapter II

The mountains rose to the west in cold white-tipped glory. They loomed in the distance beyond the forest to the right of the trail. The golden light of dawn gilded the snowy crests.

The first sunrise of my married life. Eve fought back the disturbing thought and glanced at her husband. Attached for the rest of her existence, they were beginning their relationship as such strangers. She swallowed the panicky tightening in her throat.

She studied her mate. An attractive man, not even his loose shirt disguised the muscle that came from hard work or the pleasing breadth of his shoulders. She reluctantly admitted his thick, brown hair made her fingers itch to smooth it back from his forehead. Even now, when only his profile was visible, she admired many of the features, like his straight nose.

Ever since leaving the Servant of the Kurios the evening before, Labren urged the horses forward through the night. The resulting strain hunched his torso forward and his head down. His lips pulled taut in determination, and extra lines creased the skin around his eyes and mouth.

He promised her they would stop soon after sunrise. Hours had passed since their last heated exchange and his descent into stony silence. Not the way she pictured spending her first night with her new husband. Not that she had ever considered being married. But the hope he would spare himself an extra few hours' sleep if she fought for it was incentive enough. Now his steady and pointed ignoring made her uneasy. *What kind of a man is he when angered?* Fear flickered in her heart. She was just going to have to find out for his sake. *Give me boldness, Kurios,* she prayed.

Although she did not look forward to the awkwardness of their new sleeping arrangements, he was pushing himself too hard for his own good. His limbs needed rest and time to heal. He refused to give them either. Wary of the consequences of sparking his anger further, she debated speaking again.

"Shouldn't we stop soon?" She drew his attention to the brightening skies above the foot hills to their left. "The grove of trees over there offers a perfect shelter." She pointed to a place about a mile back from the road. The vegetation grew thick enough to offer cool, dark shade from the midday sun. Also, the foliage would block their camp from the sight of any other travelers. She hoped he had stopped ignoring her. The reins shook in his hands.

"All right." He turned off the dirt way into the tall grass.

Eve let out the air she had been holding in her lungs and relaxed a little. *Thank you.* At least her husband was listening again.

Labren guided the horses around the grove to the side away from the main road. The wagon stopped under the shadow of an ancient oak. Eve jumped down. Her knees shook and threatened to give, but she ignored them as she ran around to the other side to help Labren.

He moved slowly. By the time she reached his elbow he had turned in his seat. Groaning at the screaming of his abused legs and arms, he started to gingerly move toward the ground. At first he planned to disregard Eve's offered shoulder, but his weak leg forced him to use it.

A nearby stump made a solid seat. Eve gathered a small heap of brush and then fetched the tinderbox. She gave it to him.

"We will need a small fire for cooking dinner." She returned to the wagon to gather the supplies.

Grateful for an occupation, Labren bent to the task. Eve was long in returning; so, when she did, he had let the original blaze burn down to a good cooking temperature. She prepared a simple meal of tea, bacon, and bread.

Labren watched her, feeling guilty. He had been outright rude to her. The fact her motivation was his best interest made his behavior all the more awful. Not even one day into their marriage and he was already acting like a heel, hardly God honoring behavior. His stomach clenched.

"I apologize."

His voice sounded harsh to his ears. She looked up from her crouching position near the sizzling bacon.

"For what?"

Anger rose in his chest because he thought she was being difficult. He opened his mouth to retort, but the mild confusion on her face brought the words to a halt. Her expression quickly changed into hurt. She moved the food around in the pan.

"Oh, that. You are forgiven."

"Thank you." His words sounded stiff.

She removed the bacon from the fire. "You're welcome."

Labren still regretted his behavior as he ate his meal. Also, what had absorbed her attention enough to wipe everything else from her mind? When he finished his food, his head and eyes grew heavy. Fighting to stay awake he tried to stand. Before he realized she moved, Eve was next to him, draping his good arm across her thin shoulders. Unusually strong for her size, she bore his weight steadily. He would not have thought her small frame was so sturdy. Thankfully, appearances deceived in this instance; he needed her support.

They crossed the clearing together. With her assistance, he climbed into the wagon bed. He discovered that she had made up their one mattress with pillows and quilts. She helped him out of his jacket, shirt, pants, boots, and socks. Then she left him to climb under the blankets. Labren did not note the chill earlier in the day. Now with only his under things and hose protecting him from the cold he remembered it was mid-November. Winter was coming.

He slipped into the soft bedclothes. Sleep claimed him quickly. His last thought was a question. *How are we going to get through the mountains in snow?*

Huddling against the sudden wind, Eve briskly cleared the meal mess. She almost longed for the shelter of the wagon when she finished. The smell of winter came in frigid gusts. The sky, which had been clear earlier, filled with dark clouds. Eve figured the overdue winter weather would debut during the day. Even then she was not eager to encounter the cold and wet.

After stowing the pan under the seat, she climbed over it and between the canvas flaps that blocked out the wind. The air inside still bit at her hands and face. She studied her sleeping husband. His long legs and out-flung arm took up most of the bed. Maybe if she moved it a little, she would have space to lie without touching him. The temperature dropped even as she removed her dress and petticoat. She pulled back the covers and climbed under the quilts.

Beneath the covers, Labren radiated a tempting aura of

heat. She adjusted herself for sleep. He moved just as she found a comfortable position on the lumpy mattress. At first she thought he was awake, but as his hand slid to touch her shoulder she grew uncertain. Holding her breath, she waited to see what he would do. He rolled over and put his arm loosely about her waist. This trapped her on her side with her back to his front. She tensed, but he seemed to have fallen into peaceful slumber. His breath tickled the hairs at the nape of her neck while his warmth soaked into her back. Resigned to their new position, she closed her eyes and tried to sleep. She, at least, needed to be rested.

Labren waited until her body and breathing indicated she had fallen asleep. Then he moved. From the sound of the wind, they needed each other to stay warm tonight. Once he was satisfied she was not going to freeze, he let the comfort of sleep claim him again.

Eve awoke before Labren. With difficulty she extracted herself from his embrace. She crept from the refuge of the bedclothes and quickly dressed. After checking that Labren remained warm, she slipped between the cover flaps and into the chill of the evening.

A light blanket of snow frosted the ground. Eve's shoes offered little protection from even this dusting. By the time she started a small fire, she could no longer feel her toes. Shaking against the cold, she broke the thin layer of ice in the water bucket and poured the liquid beneath into the kettle. She set the pot close to the fire, soaking up the warmth of the flame. The potatoes would be a welcome treat if she baked them in the coals.

She quietly climbed back into the wagon to find Labren awake and digging through one of the trunks. He looked up when she appeared. "Where are the bundles...?" He clamored across the crowded wagon bed to claim her hands. "You must be frozen. What are you thinking going out without an extra layer?" He massaged her frigid fingers with his gloved ones.

"I don't have one." Her teeth knocked together as she spoke.

"Yes, you do." Frustrated at the clumsiness of his gloves, he removed the offending items. He warmed her fingers with one of his large hands while reaching toward a nearby trunk simultaneously. "I bought outer clothing that I thought would possibly fit you when we were in town. Now where are those packages?"

Before Eve could protest, he bundled her into a coat two sizes too big. He produced mittens and boots, both of which were larger than needed. Only after he had found woolen socks and a scarf for each of them, did he stop to examine her.

Eve immediately spoke up. "It is not cold enough out to merit all this. Besides I could not possibly do chores in these; I would ruin them." She held out the gloves for his inspection.

"Nonsense." Labren waded through the mess again, so that he towered over her. "You will wear them for as long as I say you need them. I bought them for our use." Eve indignantly straightened to his commanding tone. She was about to speak her mind. Labren stopped her by placing his warm fingers against her cold mouth.

"I try not to issue commands very often, Eve. But when I do, I believe I have a right to your obedience. Let me be a good husband in at least this way." His face was kind; however Eve sensed he would not back down on this point.

"I will use them. I need to finish preparing breakfast." She gathered the potatoes and climbed over the side. She hated to admit it, but she needed the extra protection the coat gave against the wind.

Two weeks passed in dragging monotony. Traveling by night, sleeping by day, Labren watched the pace wear down his body and the concern grow in Eve's eyes. Every time she redressed his wounds or glanced his way, her worry pulled at her brow. He hated seeing the tightening of her mouth and her turning away to hide what she thought.

So, when they discovered a traveling caravan one morning as they searched for a campsite for the night, he made a decision.

"We should join them if we can."

He pulled at the reins and guided their horses over to the side of the road. Ten wagons camped about twenty feet away. Amber and gold cooking fires lit the gray dawn within the circle. Men and women moved around them, most likely eating their morning meals.

Handing Eve the leads, he climbed down from the seat.

"What about our rest? You have been driving all night."

He waved away her objection and strode off toward the wagons. "Keep the horses still. I will be right back."

His arrival at the fringe of the camp caused a small stir.

"What business do you have here?" a young man demanded, stepping out from the shadow of the closest wagon. He stood at least as tall as Labren, but still had the lankiness of youth about his limbs.

"I wish to speak to the wagon master regarding joining your caravan."

"You come alone?" The man looked past Labren to Eve.

"No, my wife," the word still sounded foreign to his tongue, "and I are traveling toward Ana City. Where are you headed?"

"As far as Canktinton, on the border."

Labren nodded. "I am familiar with the area. May we travel with you?"

The man glanced over at Eve again. "We'll find room, but it will cost you. We don't have extra supplies."

Labren frowned, but shook his head. "We brought our own." The pointed interest in Eve rankled his instincts, but the dull ache in his limbs overwhelmed them.

The man shrugged. "Father will still insist on payment." Then he turned and strode toward the central fire circle.

The young man, Ulysses, was correct. His father demanded an outrageous fee, but Labren was compelled to pay for the peace of mind. He read the signs of his earlier pursuers closing in on them: strangers asking questions, strained looks when purchasing supplies, and an occasional patrol riding past them. Any time now they would connect him to the disappearance of a slave girl. The additional cover of traveling in a caravan might help. They traveled slowly with all the women and children, the opposite of what the trackers would expect.

"So, where are you from, little mouse?"

Eve lifted her head from scrubbing the dinner pot. Her hands shook from exhaustion. They had now traveled a full day and night without rest. Her eyes protested at the idea of focusing. The wagon master's son stood over her, grinning in a way he clearly thought disarming.

Eve returned to scrubbing.

"Must be somewhere north."

Eve blinked hazily and tried to think about what she needed to do next.

"Now is not the time to visit, Ulysses." Labren's voice broke through her drifting thoughts. "We have had a long day."

Ulysses shrugged. "See you folks tomorrow."

Labren watched him leave through narrowed eyes. Eve felt vaguely uneasy.

"Try to avoid that one, Eve. He is trouble."

She nodded. Tears rose unbidden. She was so intent on not letting them fall she jumped when Labren's hand closed around hers.

"Come to bed. The rest can wait until tomorrow."

Obediently, Eve lay down the scrub brush and dumped the water out of the pot. She didn't want to let the kettle rust again considering the elbow effort to clean it initially.

After stumbling up into the wagon with Labren's help, she fell asleep before he blew out the lantern.

A patrol passed the wagon train in a cacophony of yells, hoof beats, and swearing. Perched on the seat, Labren hunched deeper into his scarf and coat and prayed they didn't look back.

"Are you certain they are still searching for you?" Eve asked from her place next to him.

"Positive."

She turned to watch one of the children running to catch another.

He almost heard the unanswered inquiries whirling around her brain. His grip tightened on the reins. After four weeks of marriage, she should have asked one of the questions, but she didn't. Instead, she avoided his gaze and concentrated on knitting something. One of the other women taught her a week ago. Now she hid behind a skein of wool, wooden needles, and a growing knot of something.

Closing his eyes, he sighed. Every night she clung to the distance between them until she relaxed into sleep. Each meal swiftly became a study in stunted conversation. He wanted more, but he feared there never would be. At least she treated the whelp, Ulysses, the same way. *No*, he corrected himself, *she treats him*

23

worse. Her reception of his advances grew downright frigid.

"How much farther?" she asked.

Shaking off his grim mood, Labren glanced around. The long dusty road lay out before them, winding through rolling hills covered by forests and fields. "What was the name of the town at the last crossroads?"

"Overkan, I believe."

"Then we have another month." He glanced her way to judge her reaction. She frowned and stared up at the grey sky.

"The snow will not hold out that long."

"Making camp!" Ulysses called out as he rode back along the line of wagons. Their wagon brought up the tail of the caravan. "Camp is in sight," he informed them as he pulled up next to them and flashed Eve a brilliant grin. He then heeled his tired horse, forcing him to lunge forward half mad into a gallop and leave them in a cloud of dust.

"Inconsiderate fool," Labren muttered.

"Idiot." Eve coughed.

Labren's chest warmed with hope as he guided their vehicle into its place. She wasn't a fool or interested in a fool. The sensation lived a very brief life.

Not an hour later, his stomach tightened like a vice. With sharp eyes he scanned the camp. Eve approached their fireside with their daily ration of water. Ulysses hid behind the wagon closest to theirs. The leer of the wagon master's son made his hands itch for a weapon.

Eve's face brightened and she smiled at him as she crossed the middle of the circle. Labren tried to force himself to smile and not show his worry. He knew he was not convincing her.

"What is the matter?" She poured some of the water into the kettle.

"I will tell you later." He made a big show of walking to the tethered horses. He struggled not to limp although it aggravated his leg. Just as he expected, once his back turned, the scoundrel eased his way over to where Eve stirred their supper. While Labren checked the hooves of his animals, Ulysses offered to cut the bread for her.

To Eve's credit, she pushed strands of loose hair back behind her ears and coolly declined his offer. Not to be rejected completely, the man insisted on lifting the kettle from over the fire.

Deciding he had seen enough, Labren hobbled the horse and turned back to his wagon. Long before he arrived, Ulysses left.

Taking in Eve's pale cheeks and lowered eyes, Labren decided he would deal with this problem before bed. Even if it meant they parted with the caravan, he needed to speak with the wagon master about Ulysses. He would wait until a private moment to speak with Eve.

His wife's hands shook when she handed him his stew.

Eve worked at cleaning up the meal mess as Labren walked over to the main fire that always burned in the center of camp. Her mind raced and her hands moved by rote.

All attempts to block out Ulysses' face from her memory proved futile. The way he leered at her twisted her stomach. She gulped back the bile in her throat. The proposal he offered made her want a bath.

Labren's silence did not comfort her at all. An unreasonable feeling that she shamed him grew in her chest. She tried to occupy her mind elsewhere, but found herself dwelling upon the tight panic growing in her stomach.

She finished the chores more quickly than usual and dumped out the dirty dishwater while the dying fire still glowed. Even though Labren did not return from the main fireside until most of the stars appeared, Eve climbed into their wagon to begin making their bed for the night.

After lighting the lantern, she placed it on the top of their clothes' chest. Its golden-red glow deepened the shadows behind the various boxes and trunks filling the floor. She began to wrestle their mattresses out from their wooden box when she heard a sound. She paused mid-motion to listen.

The stride of the person approaching was clear in spite of the distant scolding of the mothers calling the children to bed. Somehow she knew the man outside the wagon was not her husband.

Avoiding making shadows on the canvas, Eve slipped behind the half empty chest. Moments before he began to hoist himself over the wheel hub, she tucked herself under the partially unpacked mattress. She stopped breathing as he pushed aside the flap and entered.

For what seemed like an eternity to Eve, Ulysses stood and

25

surveyed the room before him. He stepped toward her. Eve swallowed a gasp as her heart thundered in her ears.

"I saw you come in here, Eve." Annoyance tinged his tone. She had forced him to seek her. "There were wild animals wandering the camp. I came to check on you." He took two steps to the middle of the floor. The toes of his dirty and scuffed work boots appeared near her head.

She needed to breathe soon or pass out. What would he do then? She did not want to find out. Timidly she let some of the stale air out her nose. Then he surprised her by moving toward the mattress. The remaining air rushed out.

With a cry of triumph, Ulysses lunged for her. "I have you!"

Eve screamed. She burst forth. Not bothering with circumventing the obstacles between her and the back of the wagon, she leaped for the opening in the canvas. She made it only to fall to the hard ground about five feet below. She scrambled to her feet and plowed right into her husband's arms.

Labren had been walking back from his brief talk with the wagon master. He informed the older man of his intention to turn off the trail at the next crossroads. The wagon master refused to refund any of the money they paid. In the end, Labren decided the argument was not worth the effort. He had changed their plans and the new destination would hopefully offer them room and board for the winter in exchange for his services.

The events of the afternoon gave him no choice. They could not travel over the mountains by themselves. Danger hunted both of them if they continued with this group much longer. Besides, his body demanded rest. His injuries were healing more slowly than desired. He needed a break from the draining work of travel.

His speech to the Professor ran through his head. Then Eve's cry startled him out of his thoughts. His legs quickened their pace. The wagon's looming shadow touched his feet when Eve crashed into him. His arms encircled her as his bad leg complained at the sudden strain. By sheer determination, he stayed upright.

While holding the trembling body of his wife, he spotted the figure of Ulysses creeping away. A knot formed in his stomach.

Tonight Eve required all the comfort he could give. Tomorrow, he intended to have a 'talk' with that boy. The rascal would never pursue another man's wife again. Then they were leaving. The school was only hours away. He remembered where to go and how to get them there.

Soothingly Labren ushered his Eve into the wagon.

Much later, he lay on his side watching her sleep. As he watched the rise and fall of her shoulders, he wondered at the swiftness his job of cherishing and protecting his wife had changed from duty to delight. She was an amazing woman. A strange combination of intelligence, caring, and stubbornness, she constantly surprised him with her strength. He glimpsed her immobilized by fear. The same fear, until tonight, distanced her from him. How ironic she clung to him for comfort and protection. He hoped she would trust him more now.

Adjusting his pillow and turning to his other side, he settled his aching limbs into a better position. He rubbed his injured thigh. As exhaustion claimed the last of his tired thoughts, he grew dimly aware of Eve curling her small warmth against his back. For the first night in almost thirteen years, his sleep was dreamless.

The next morning Labren woke to the sounds of camp breaking. Thankfully Eve still slept. He extracted himself from bed and dressed. By the time he swung down, the women around them were up to their elbows in the morning's dishes and the men occupied preparing their horses.

Finding Ulysses took him ten minutes.

"Ulysses," he said as he approached the wagon of a young family with a pretty daughter. The boy turned from flirting to grimace at Labren.

"What?"

"I have business with you."

"What business could you have with me?" His tone oozed confident bravo for the benefit of his audience. The girl watched doe-eyed. "You broke off with my father, as I understand."

"I did. The issue isn't with him. It is with you. You assaulted my wife."

"She asked for it."

A harsh laugh tore from Labren's throat. "She didn't."

"Don't be so sure, old man. Just because she is married to

27

you, you think she is dead to the charms of men her own age."
Ulysses ran a hand through his long hair and looked pointedly at
Labren's weaker leg. "She needed a real man, someone who
doesn't need to be waited on or assisted in and out of a wagon."

"I will only warn you once. Prepare to defend yourself."

"You wouldn't dare." Ulysses presented his back.

Labren didn't pause a second. He stepped forward, grabbed
the young man's shoulder, and let his fist fly. It collided with the
boy's jaw with a satisfying crack.

The girl screamed.

"See here." Her father protested as he rounded the wagon.

Ignoring them both, Labren applied his second fist. Pain
sluiced up his arm, but he bore it. The boy wavered before sitting
heavily in the dirt. Blood dripped from his broken nose and off his
chin. He stared up at Labren in shock.

"I told you once to leave Eve alone. That should have been
enough." Satisfied, Labren limped away with the sound of
Ulysses' angry howl in his ears.

"Move out!" the wagon master called from the front of the
line. The caravan began to roll. Labren glanced over his shoulder
in time to catch the young woman's father rushing her away.
Within moments their wagon joined the formation. Ulysses, still
nursing his oozing face, scrambled after them.

Labren returned to his wagon. Isolated in the barren
expanse of an abandoned camp, he savored the overwhelming
wave of relief. His leg throbbed and his arm screamed, but Eve
was safe again.

They needed to start soon to reach the school before dark.
Considering and rejecting the idea of waking Eve, he decided to
prepare breakfast. He would save Eve the work and get them
moving faster once she woke. Besides he needed to work off the
adrenaline high thrumming through him.

Eve opened her eyes to yellow brightness. Morning
sunshine touched the canvas above her face. She stared at the
ceiling for a moment. Then it occurred to her that she had
overslept. Before she could wonder why Labren did not wake her,
he climbed between the flaps.

"Oh, good." He stood to his full height in the center of the
wagon and smiled down at her. "Glad you are awake. I wanted to

ask where the kettle is. The fire is perfect for boiling water, and I need a large cup of moracca."

Eve pointed out the beaten copper pot. He disappeared, and she hurried out of bed and into her clothes. She rushed to pack away their bedding, silently scolding herself for sleeping late the whole while. As she grabbed her wraps, she wondered why she didn't hear the other wagoneers or their animals.

When she straightened from her jump to the ground, she realized the reason for the silence. They were nowhere to be seen. Swallowing a sudden panicky feeling, she turned toward the reassuring sight of the breakfast fire and her husband.

"They left at dawn." Labren fixed his attention on the oatmeal as he poured it into their wooden bowls. "We were leaving their company soon anyway. I figured it best if we parted sooner than planned." He looked up briefly as he handed her the steaming bowl. "I settled accounts with the wagon master last night. I dealt with the loose ends this morning."

When Eve did not comment, Labren paused in his movement, spoon suspended. "I did not realize until now that I had not discussed any of my plans with you."

He resumed stirring his breakfast. Eve stole a peek at him and then at the fire. The kettle threatened to overflow. The mouthful on her spoon went in her mouth. She hurriedly set down her bowl and reached for the black handle of the kettle.

Labren started a bit in surprise at her sudden movement. He watched while she finished rescuing his moracca.

"Do you want some?" she asked. Their eyes met and Eve read conflict in his. He held out his mug and she filled it. "You know our destination. I am going with you, so why do you need to ask me?"

"Eve." His voice shook. "You are my spouse, not my slave." He continued haltingly as she returned the kettle to its place and picked up her oatmeal. "Freedom means you should have some say in where you go or stay. Sorry I have been treating you like a servant."

Eve prepared to protest, but changed her mind and returned to her porridge. Labren perceived marriage differently than most men. The few couples she witnessed seemed to portray the role of the wife as a glorified slave. She wanted to please Labren and the best way at the moment was to listen to his plans. She did not point out the fact she possessed no other choice.

"What is the plan?" Her question seemed to startle him out of his thoughts.

"Before the events yesterevening..." He started to clean up as he spoke. "I planned for us to separate from the caravan this afternoon. My wounds have not been doing very well lately. And, I was beginning to second guess the wisdom of continuing over the mountains this late in the year.

"Instead we are going to turn off and seek shelter for the winter at a school I know of. The headmaster is a friend and I think I can convince him to let me work there for the winter."

He reached for Eve's bowl, but she shook her head. "I will finish up."

He willingly handed her the wash rag and moved off toward the wagon. He worked on hitching the horses. Eve threw out the dishwater and tucked the pot under the canvas behind the bench. Then she waited for Labren.

He paused after settling himself on the hard wood of the seat. "I want you to know Ulysses will never approach another man's wife without thinking twice." She did not ask for an explanation and he did not offer one. She was just thankful that he was not injured, and she did not have to encounter Ulysses again.

Chapter III

The shelter of trees ended abruptly. Ice flecks masquerading as snowflakes bit into Eve's face while the wind froze her already cold nose. The violent gusts blew across the road, blinding them with a sheet of white.

"Almost there. This is the property line. Only another mile to the house," Labren yelled above the screaming wind.

Eve raised her head and peered ahead. Snow whipped sideways in the frigid wind. The horses' tails disappeared in the haze of heaving white. She ducked her face back down into her scarf. A rush of fear carried her stomach into her throat.

A castle-like manor, an exclusive school for the nobility and future leaders of the world, the images summoned by Labren's partial descriptions did not comfort her. The storm interrupted their conversation hours ago. Now he devoted all of his attentions and waning energy keeping them on the road. Eve struggled to dwell on encouraging thoughts of a warm fire, hot food, and dry clothes. A lump formed in her throat.

A huge gray-black structure loomed vaguely through the constantly changing mass of the snow. Even when they pulled to a stop near the door, Eve could not make out much of the building beyond the meager shelter of the porch.

She glanced over at Labren and all fears of who might be inside vanished. He clumsily wrapped the reins around their hook and began a slow climb down. Eve rushed to beat him to the ground, but she was late reaching his side. He rested for a moment leaning against the side of the wagon.

"I can knock," she offered.

Waving her away, he hobbled toward the door. He pulled on the cord to announce their arrival and then sagged against the wall beyond. Eve moved quickly to his side. He welcomed her offered support with a grimace of pain when she moved his arm to her shoulders.

She looked up at his face. "What hurts?"

He had not answered when the door opened. Immediately a

woman drew them inside and closed the door firmly behind them. Eve began to gather her bearings when someone exclaimed, "Trahern!" Labren's leg gave out and Eve put all her effort to keeping him off the floor.

A tall young man came toward them from across the large hall. Eve looked up at him pleadingly, not managing to form the words to ask for help. Labren's full weight began to settle against her as his consciousness wavered. The man sprinted the last steps, catching Labren's snow-covered shoulder as he sagged forward.

"Get the Professor."

The middle-aged woman hurried away. Eve searched desperately for a chair. Her helper smoothly reached out his foot and pulled the nearest chair to where they could deposit Labren in it.

"Abrigail will fetch the Professor. He will know what to do. Where does it hurt?" The question was directed at Labren.

Labren hunched over. Eve feared for a moment that he lost his hold on awareness. She knelt on the floor at his feet so she could see his face. Even in the shadows, she could make out the tautness of his mouth and his tightly closed eyes. She reached up to push his hair back so she could see him better. He caught her hand and held it tightly.

"Am I hallucinating again?" he asked hoarsely, the words barely discernable. She hesitated, not sure how to answer.

"What hurts?"

"Everything." His voice again rasped weakly. She moved her free hand to his leg. The young man knelt next her as she began to try to loosen his boot with one hand.

"Here let me." The man's warmer fingers made quick work of the laces.

"He was wounded about two months ago." Eve informed him as he worked. The man nodded his head in acknowledgment. He drew the boot off slowly. Eve did not try to remove her hand from Labren's grasp even though he tightened it painfully. "Please be gentle." She meant to caution the stranger, but Labren loosened his grip on her fingers.

With a steady care, the foot emerged from the boot. Dimly aware of the sounds of others arriving, Eve flinched at Labren's cry of pain.

"He needs to be moved to a bedroom." A new voice cut

through Eve's concentration. A pair of new, large hands guided her to her feet and three men joined the first.

With swiftness and grace, the four of them lifted Labren. Then without a word, they hauled him in the direction of the sweeping staircase to the second floor. Somehow in the shuffle, Labren lost hold of her hand. Abrigail intervened instead, restraining her by the arm.

"You look beat, child. Come let me help you out of those wet things."

Eve let her take the cloak, but she refused to be drawn down the hall.

"I must go with my husband."

Abrigail dropped her grasp on Eve's arm with a harsh gasp. Ignoring the woman's obvious shock, Eve bolted for the base of the stairs. Labren's escort was just disappearing at the top. Her mad dash gained her half the flight before she encountered a young man coming down.

"He is calling for an Eve." The dark skinned lad's striking blue eyes studied her face for a moment. "Are you Eve?"

"Yes."

He stepped aside. "I will show you where."

Relieved, Eve followed him up the stairs and down the hall. The first door on the left side of the second hallway stood open. She entered only to be confronted by Labren's escort. All four men looked at her curiously, but none of them moved to restrain her.

"Where is Eve?" The distress in Labren's voice made her heart ache. He lay on a huge bed that dominated the far wall. Ignoring the formidable looking crowd in the room, Eve strode straight to his side and claimed his hand.

"I am here." His long, cold fingers closed around hers like a vise. The trust in his eyes gave her the strength to turn and face the silent watchers. "I will need boiling water, clean bandages, and some quilts." Her voice shook. Thankfully the man that had helped them earlier quickly dispatched the youngest two boys to fetch her supplies.

"If you describe what is wrong, perhaps I can help." An older gentleman met her questioning glance with a warm smile. His wise, sharp scrutiny and air of calm confidence and warmth soothed her fear a bit.

Labren squeezed her hand. "Trust them, Eve." She obeyed

and stepped away from the bed.

The man leaned over Labren, flashing a warm smile Eve's way. "My students and friends call me Professor Olof." His hands touched Labren's forehead. "You are...?"

"Eve."

He nodded. "Han, I will need your assistance undressing him. The rest of you may leave." Despite the fact his voice never rose above the even timber of private conversation, the room cleared before Eve could protest the man's intent.

"But..." She struggled to form the words. The room swam. Her heart pounded in her chest.

Professor Olof paused in his examination of Labren to study her face. "Han, perhaps a chair for Eve would be wise. I am not sure she will remain standing much longer."

Eve's knees wobbled. "Deep breaths, miss," Han coached as he slipped the chair under her legs. "Trahern will be just fine. Leave him to the Professor."

"But..."

Han leaned down and took her hand. "Concentrate on calming down," he instructed. "You can watch everything from here. Trahern needs you well. It won't help if you faint."

Eve agreed, but she carefully retracted her fingers from his grasp.

"Healing hampered by exhaustion." Professor Olof straightened to his full height. "How long has it been since the first injury?"

"About a month," Eve said.

A crease appeared between his thick eyebrows. "I would have expected more signs of healing." Labren stirred on the bed and muttered something Eve couldn't hear. Apparently Professor Olof did. "Intense travel." His brow raised. "That would definitely slow healing. I assume very little rest was involved."

Labren answered again.

"Then I think you should thank your lovely wife for the fact you still have all your limbs. Sleep now. We can discuss the rest tomorrow. I assume you will need assistance undressing and I doubt Eve will be up for the task. For her sake let Han assist you." Professor Olof came around the end of the bed and approached her as Han took his place at Labren's side. "Now for you."

Eve eyed him warily. "I am fine."

"Hardly, child. You are pale as the snow outside and your hands are shaking. When did you last eat?" He probed her wrist with long worn fingers.

"This morning but..."

"Shh..." he admonished. Tilting his head to the side as though listening for her pulse, his lips moved, breathing the counts as her blood pulsed beneath his cool fingers. Then dropping her hand, he caught her face between his hands and studied her features, running fingers down her cheeks to check the whites of her eyes.

"Hmm... A bit undernourished, but we can fix that soon enough. Food, bed, and we will catch up on explanations tomorrow." He straightened with a dismissive grunt and turned to Han. "I will send up food, but see they go to bed right after eating."

Eve obediently ate a silent meal, but Labren couldn't manage more than a bite before falling asleep. Before Han cleared away the meal, Eve had joined Labren on the bed. She snuggled against his overwarm body, too weary to care that there was another in the room. Oblivion came before the door closed.

Slowly Eve awoke. It took her a few moments to remember why she could not hear the wind or the sounds of a waking camp. Instead time moved to Labren's steady breathing. Images of the stressful night before jumped before her mind's eye. Resisting the urge to move and check Labren's temperature, Eve instead placed her hand over his where it encircled her waist.

Labren shifted slightly bringing Eve's thoughts back to the present.

"You awake?" His voice rasped with sleep.

"Yes."

He tightened his arm around her waist.

"I thought you were still sleeping," she explained.

"I wish." He released a sigh laced with sadness. "I need to tell you some things about my past before you find them out from a different source."

Eve sat up to give him distance. Somehow she knew this would require her undivided attention. Labren rolled onto his back and looked up at her before continuing.

"My real full name is Trahern Marcus Theodoric. I am the

eldest son of the King of Anavrea."

A prince? The thought rested against her mind, too foreign to sink beneath the surface.

Pushing himself up onto his elbows, he began to swing his legs off the bed. "This," he gestured to the room and implied the entire building, "is the school where I spent my winters from right after I turned ten until my twentieth birthday."

Focusing on his movements instead of his words, Eve quickly made her way around the bed and stood in front of him.

"You can tell me all this while you are still in bed. You are weak and your body needs rest."

"I have no intention of..." A knock on the door interrupted Labren's protest.

"Prince or not." Eve went to answer. "You are not getting out of bed."

She opened the door and found the man that had introduced himself as Han the night before. He must have heard her last few words because his blue eyes danced in amusement. He flashed a friendly smile at her, before looking past her to Labren.

"I see you have met your match," he called over her shoulder to Labren. "May I come in?" He winked at Eve. "I am interested in watching this."

Eve did not even look to see if Labren wanted company before stepping back to give Han room to pass. She trusted Han enough to know he would help her keep Labren in bed. On her own, she didn't know if she would be able to persuade the invalid to remain on his back. As weak as he was, Labren was twice her size and could easily overpower her strength.

"So, Trahern." Han crossed the room to the foot of the bed. "Where did you manage to find such a beautiful companion?" His eyes weighed Labren's dark circles, pale face, sagging shoulders, and slightly labored breathing as he continued to speak. "I see your taste in women has improved since we last met."

Labren grimaced. "It has been a long time, Atluer." Pausing in reaching for his boots, Labren glared at Han. "As I remember, your taste in the gentler sex was even worse than mine. At least, Trina did not try to kill me."

Eve realized that she had never experienced the full power of Labren's anger. The air in the room suddenly felt thicker. Han met his piercing gaze and held it. Both men had hit their mark.

"Professor Olof sent me up to fetch Eve and make sure that you were staying in bed." Not breaking his gaze from Labren's, Han turned slightly toward Eve. "The Professor's study is on the first floor, first door on the left when you go under the stairs toward the back of the house." Han settled in the chair opposite Labren. "I will make sure he does not go anywhere while you are gone."

Eve hesitated and looked at Labren. He tore his eyes away from Han and smiled weakly at her. "The Professor does not like to wait. You should go."

Turning reluctantly, Eve left the room. Her last glimpse as she closed the door behind her was of Labren swinging his legs back up onto the bed.

A few moments later, Eve closed the study door behind her with great care. The deep red of the carpet met her eyes as she turned toward the desk on the other side of the room.

"Come in and sit down," a warm voice urged her from the other side of the room. "I will be done with this in a moment."

While she slowly crossed the short distance to one of the chairs sitting opposite the huge oak desk, Eve stole a quick look at the man behind it. A man's head covered in salt and pepper hair bent over a stack of forms. She judged him to be quite old. Even though the rest of him was hidden behind the desk, she remembered that he was tall and thin, but there was no trace of frailty in his thinness. It was not long before she found a pair of warm brown eyes regarding her with an honesty she did not expect in one so old.

"You definitely look better than last night. I am probably safe in assuming that you slept well last night."

Eve immediately dropped her eyes respectfully and nodded.

He rose and walked around to the front of the desk as he spoke. "I wanted to talk to you alone before speaking with Trahern." He paused and waited for her to lift her eyes from his shoes to his face. When she met his eyes he continued.

"I do not know how he got that leg wound and I figured I would get a straighter answer out of you. Trahern has a tendency to under evaluate his injuries. I also wanted make sure that you did not have any that needed tending also."

Eve shook her head and dropped her eyes.

"If you do not quit dropping your eyes, you will never

37

convince anyone you aren't a slave." That statement brought her chin up. He smiled into her startled eyes. "I thought so. Has Trahern freed you?" He had crossed the room and turned his back to her by the time he finished voicing the question.

"He removed my collar."

"Are you married?"

Eve regarded his back not sure of the purpose of his questions. He turned toward her and raised an eyebrow to remind her he was waiting. "Yes," she said finally.

"Good." The Professor smiled in obvious relief. "He at least remembered that much of his studies. Now back to one of my earlier topics. Were you injured during the events that led to his injuries?"

Eve shook her head. "He had already been hurt when I met him."

The old man nodded in acknowledgment and walked across the room to take the seat next to hers. Turning so he faced her, he said, "Tell me everything you know." Seeing her suspicious reaction, he smiled. "You don't trust me."

"I do not know what Labren would wish me to say."

Her reply brought an amused smile to his eyes. "So he is going by Labren. Now that brings back memories." He leaned back in his chair and regarded the portrait on the wall behind the desk. His fingers of his left hand beat a steady tattoo on the upholstered arm of his chair. After a few moments, he turned back to her. "I will not ask you to betray your husband's trust. I will go ask him my questions."

Rising, he offered her his hand. Eve hesitantly took it. Leading her across the room to the double doors she had just entered, he opened one and guided her through into the hall.

"Come, we will go and see if Han has managed to make him behave while you were gone."

Eve needed to trot to keep up with the energetic Professor. After exiting his study, he swiftly headed to the main stairs. As she dreaded, he started to climb at a neck breaking pace. Her legs shook a bit by the time they had reached the bedroom door. She must have looked similar to how she felt because when Professor looked at her, he frowned.

"Are you all right?" He had knocked before turning to her so that his question was punctuated by Han opening the door.

"Han, did you bring them breakfast?"

Looking very ashamed, Han admitted that he had not. Sending him off with a frigid glare, Professor Olof ushered her into the room at a much slower pace. "I am dreadfully sorry for the oversight. I was so caught up in asking questions I forgot to ask how you were feeling." Depositing her in the chair that Han had just vacated, the Professor turned to Labren who was now sitting on the bench at the foot of the bed.

For a moment, neither man moved. The room filled with unspoken words. Finally Labren pushed himself slowly to his feet and extended his hand to the old man. "I believe I owe you an explanation, sir, of the events of a couple years ago."

Almost immediately the offered hand was taken and shaken with enthusiasm. "It is so good to see you, Trahern." The Professor continued as if Labren had never spoken. "It is always a joy to see a student again. Given the circumstances though, I believe that you had better explain to both of us." He gestured toward where Eve was sitting. "Unless, of course, she already knows she is married to a man that has a price on his head in at least three countries." He took in Eve's startled expression with concern. "It appears you have not."

Labren turned a stormy countenance toward his former teacher. "I have been trying to do just that, but I have been interrupted incessantly." He shot a pained look toward Eve, pleading for leniency. He took a step as if to stride away from them, but stopped short with a sharp intake of air. He reclaimed his seat cautiously.

"Would you like to tell her in private? I can step out of the room and come back later."

"No," Labren answered with a shake of his head, "I only want to go through this once."

Eve's throat tightened in dread. If the professor were not standing nearby, she would have urged Labren to go back to bed and changed the subject.

"Do you want us to wait for Han to return also? I believe you owe him an explanation as well." The elder man regarded Labren sternly.

"We have already had it out." Labren almost winced. Taking a deep breath, he raised his head and fastened his eyes on the painting behind her left shoulder.

"I have already told you that my true name is Trahern Theodoric and my true title is Prince. Before I came to this school, I spent my early childhood under the roof of Prince Hiaronical, my father's brother-in-law. I grew up there because the current queen could not stand having the son of her predecessor, my mother, underfoot. During my stay under his roof I made friends with others my age. That is where I befriended Han and Trina.

"In spite of the fact that the children of princes and slaves are not allowed to be friends, Han and I managed to get around most of those who tried to separate us. We referred to each other by nicknames to avoid questions. I was Labren and I called Han, Atluer.

"Trina was a ward of my uncle and three years my junior. We shared a passing friendship, but she considered Han beneath her. Together the three of us plagued my uncle's household.

"Shortly after my tenth birthday, my father arranged for me to attend this school. I knew if I did not take Han with me we would be separated for life, we figured out a way to smuggle him to the school. It took the Professor only two weeks to find us out."

Labren looked at Professor Olof while he continued. "Han was a fugitive, a runaway slave. The Professor, realizing I knew nothing of the laws of slavery, made arrangements with my uncle to buy Han. As punishment for our adventure, he made me study in minute detail the slavery laws of Anavrea, Braulyn, and Sardmara. To this day, I can quote most of the statutes."

A knock on the door announced the arrival of the meal.

Professor Olof let Han and the food in and served Eve himself. Eve noticed that Labren had not been given anything to eat when the older man indicated that the story should continue. "Trahern will be more liable to finish quickly if his stomach is waiting for food." Han took a seat near the door and Labren continued.

"Two days before I turned twenty, a message from my father arrived. He wanted me to come home and take my place at court. I did not want to leave, but I could not disobey my father.

"The first three years of living in my father's house I spent time in a different type of school. I learned a great deal about politics and the ways of government. During that time I also renewed my friendship with Trina. She served the Queen as a handmaiden.

"On my twenty-third birthday, my father told me I would marry within a year. I had choice of the bride, if I could find one within six months. Naturally I thought of Trina and asked her for her hand in marriage. She said yes. I was ecstatic. I joyfully told my father and he set the preparations in motion.

"The day before the wedding she met me in an alcove on the main stair and announced that she was going to elope with Lord Titolian, my father's political enemy. By morning, they were gone.

"My father grew livid. It did not sweeten his temperament when it was discovered the couple fled the country with a large portion of the treasury including items from the Queen's dowry.

"I suspected my stepmother of poisoning my father against me over the years. This time she succeeded. She accused me of plotting the theft with my bride-to-be in an attempt not to marry, which made no sense. An investigation began. New infractions appeared. The charges grew more muddled and flamboyant as the days passed. In the end I was accused of treason against the crown.

"My father refused to listen to reason even though many tried to persuade him. He banished me from the country. My half-brother, Ireic, became heir to the throne. I fled to my uncle in Braulyn. Prince Hiaronical secretly sheltered me for about a year.

"During the time that I had resided in Anavrea's capital, Ana City, Atluer gained his freedom and returned to visit his mother. While there, he met a young woman, fell in love, and married her." Labren tried to catch Han's eye, but Han concentrated on the floor. However, Eve noticed tension in his practiced slouch. Labren continued.

"When I arrived, Atluer introduced us and asked me to stay with them. Adria, his wife, decided that she liked me more than Atluer. When I made plans to move on at the end of the year, she secretly planned to follow me. The night before I left, she tried to poison Atluer and his mother. Thankfully Atluer, noticing her odd behavior, caught her. Adria told Atluer a bunch of lies. Not wanting to completely disbelieve his wife, Atluer confronted me. We exchanged harsh words and parted company." Labren paused for breath.

Han raised his head. "I found out the truth two weeks later. I saw it was too late to find Trahern, so, I came here to seek advice from the Professor. Adria died that winter in an epidemic." A sadness, very similar to the one that occasionally haunted Labren's eyes, shadowed Han's. Eve's heart ached for him.

"Meanwhile," Labren continued, "I joined the Anavrean army in Sardmara. After three years in the service, my identity was discovered and again I had to run. Some of my father's men stumbled upon me near where I met Eve. That was when I discovered my father wants me dead. They recognized me and when I ran, they tried to bring me down like an animal. If Eve had not happened upon me, they would have succeeded."

Labren's shoulders sagged.

The Professor broke the silence. "Your father is dying. The Queen is dead, but her lies have endured. He is still against you. I believe she warped him with her hatred. He is no longer sane." He stood and crossed to put a long hand on Labren's bent head as if he were a small boy again. "Ireic has been in touch with me." Labren looked up at the Professor. Hope glimmered in his eyes. "When your father dies, your brother plans to pardon you and offer you the crown." Confusion contorted Labren's face.

Abruptly the Professor lifted his hand and walked across to the far side of the room. "Until then, you can stay here. Han and I have been discussing recently that we needed another teacher." Turning without stopping, the old man marched back toward them still talking. "You would be perfect for the job. As well as paying your salary and board, I will train Eve." As he turned and chose a new course across the room, he caught Labren's surprised and puzzled expression. "We cannot have your queen acting like a meek slave." He pointed out. "Besides I am sure she will need to learn something of reading and writing as well as government and deportment."

Eve, panic closing her throat, opened her mouth to protest, but Labren had quickly risen to his feet. Taking the two steps necessary to block the elder man's way, he said. "I am not so sure that I am going to accept the crown of Anavrea."

The pain from his leg must have been awful because he trembled with the effort. Fighting for control of his limbs, he continued, "I also refuse to accept money for my services. Any teaching I do will not be worth more than our room and board."

Han reached Labren's elbow before he had finished speaking. Eve, abandoning her plate, moved to his side. She attempted to coax him to lean on her. Overwhelmed by the pain,

Labren closed his eyes and tried to gain control of his emotions.

"Please lie down." Eve had not even realized she had spoken. For a moment she was afraid he was going to refuse, but, finally, he allowed them to escort him to the bed. Once Labren settled on his back, the Professor sent Han for his supplies. Talking the whole time, he removed the old dressings and reapplied new.

When he was finished, Labren ate. Finally Professor Olof left. Han lingered a moment more.

"If you give Eve any trouble or move from that bed, I will personally tie you down so you cannot move."

Labren acknowledged the warning with a weary nod. Worry etched lines across Han's brow as he left.

The warning was not needed. By the time Eve made her way to the bed, Labren was asleep.

With her mind full of Labren's past, she laid down with the intention of only resting a few moments. Sleep claimed her quickly. She barely felt Labren's seeking hand finding her and drawing her close.

Eve woke to the rumbling of her stomach. The sun's after light had faded the bedroom to monochrome when she finally opened her eyes. Labren did not stir as she eased from the bed and dressed. Someone had brought up their clothing chest. The clothes were wrinkled, but clean.

The scent of campfire smoke and grass filled her nose as she pulled the last layer over her head. Ulysses and the constant fear of capture flickered through her thoughts, but she shoved it away. Labren seemed to think they were safe here. She trusted him to know. After all, he was the one who had been living on the run for years.

She crept to the door in the last of the fading light and let herself out into the hall.

"How is he?"

Her heart jumped. Hand to chest, she labored to calm it.

"I am sorry," Han immediately apologized. "I thought you saw me."

She shook her head. "He is sleeping."

"Any fever?"

"Mild. It usually comes at night."

Han signaled his understanding. "And you?" Concern

written clearly in his eyes, he smiled down at her.

"Hungry."

"Well, that I can help you with. The kitchen is always well stocked. If Abrigail is about, she will fix you something. If she isn't, I will see that you don't starve. Come this way." Catching her elbow with his hand, he gently guided her in the direction of the stairs.

The sweeping staircase from the second to the first floor dropped them in the center of the two story entrance hall. Passing beneath its arch, he led her past the closed double doors of Professor Olof's study. A bar of dim light on the sill signaled life beyond.

"The Professor is probably writing letters or reading." Han jutted his chin toward the right. "This floor is mostly classrooms. But, back here is the kitchen, the best room in the house." The hallway opened into a huge room with floor to ceiling windows along the back wall. "Through here." Han backed into a heavy swinging door and pulled her through into a spacious, immaculate kitchen.

"I don't see Abrigail so it looks like you get to taste some of my cooking." He abandoned her in the center of the room to check on the fire casting a rosy glow across the worn hearthstones. "Come sit by the fire and rest. You still look a bit tired. I am not much of a cook, I must warn you. You are in for cheese and toast. I hope you don't mind."

Her stomach rumbled loudly in reply.

He smiled. "I will take that as a request for speed."

Within moments he had her settled in a heavy, comfortable chair, feet toward the fire and the smell of warm bread filling her nose.

"So, tell me about yourself."

She eyed him suspiciously. Labren indicated he trusted these men, but her habits and instincts of self-preservation were hard to ignore.

"Okay, tell me about how you got here."

She summarized the events of the last few months. Han, she discovered, was a great listener. He waited patiently for her to form her thoughts, asked the right questions, and prodded her to continue when she slowed. She discovered herself saying much more about her worries regarding Ulysses and the hunters pursuing

Labren than she intended. When she finally halted her ramblings with a large chunk of bread oozing over in cheddar, Han leaned back in his chair and contemplated the dancing flames in silence. She swallowed her bite and he spoke.

"I am certain Ulysses' reach will not extend this far. A member of a traveling caravan has little clout with locals of the towns he passes through. I doubt he will even bring up charges against Trahern, whatever it was Trahern did to him.

"The patrols are another problem completely." He glared at the glowing logs. "I will have to speak with Professor." He glanced at her and caught her worried expression. "We will protect him, Eve. Trahern is among friends. We will protect you both.

Lessons began for Eve the next morning. In an empty classroom on the first floor, Professor Olof set her to learning how to walk like a queen, at least that is what he called it. She thought the contortions made her resemble a woman with a rod stuck up her back.

"Chin higher." His voice echoed in the hollow space. The wooden floors and bare windows offered nothing to muffle the sound. "Shoulders back, stomach in, smaller steps, you must look as though you are above the world."

But I am not. She obediently attempted to glide up and down the row of desks with her nose pointed at the far wall, but her heart didn't agree with the new posture. Fear seeped in. If Labren became king, she would always have to be like this. Years of parading for unfriendly eyes loomed before her. At least as a slave, she could do what she needed to avoid the malevolent attention that frequently turned her way. As a queen, she would never be allowed to hide. Labren would depend on her to keep up the act. A lump formed in her throat and tears pressed behind it.

"What do you think you are doing, Master Trahern," Abrigail demanded outside in the hallway.

Professor Olof strode the doorway.

"Trahern, you will never heal if you don't rest."

Labren's muffled reply sounded weak. Eve darted to Olof's side. Sagging against the wall, face whitewashed and eyes closed, Labren took slow measured breaths.

"I underestimated the effort of going downstairs." His eyes opened. Glassy, they focused on her reluctantly as though fighting

45

him. "How go the lessons?"

"Back to bed." Professor Olof signaled to Abrigail. "Go fetch Han. Trahern will need carrying back up those stairs." The woman disappeared and Olof turned steely blue eyes on Labren. "Can you walk?"

"I made it here, didn't I?" He shoved away from the wall, but the bravado ended there. Eve and Olof barely caught him as he sank toward the floor. Maneuvering him into a chair took even more effort and skill. Once there, Labren settled his head in his hands and didn't move.

"Now don't be a fool." Olof retrieved his book and returned. "You are helping no one, least of all yourself with these games. Han and I will return you to your bed and you will stay there until I tell you that you can rise, understood?"

"I will not spend the next month on my back in a bed." Labren raised his head and straightened to glare at Olof. "My leg might be weak, but my mind is active. You take Eve away, Han has his duties, and I expect everyone else has occupations more pressing than entertaining an invalid."

"I will have books brought down from the library. You will only be bedbound for a few days." Olof waved the volume in his hand for emphasis. "Just pick a subject and we will collect what you need."

"Books are well enough, but I need some interaction. You know I have never been able to read for more than a few hours without a need for a break. My mind will not stay focused that long."

Olof grunted as Han appeared around the corner. "I will see what I can do."

"So, he escaped." Crossing his arms, Han regarded Labren with a light twist of his mouth. "Have you been chasing skirts?"

"No." An edge to Labren's voice hinted at anger.

"So, where do you want the miscreant?"

"In his bed." Olof waved Eve into the classroom. "Back to work, Eve. You are doing passably well with the walk. I want you to attempt a curtsey now. Remember, keep your back straight."

"Olof, books?" Labren called from the hallway.

"Han, will you see about someone fetching some reading material for Trahern?" The professor pointed to Eve's feet. "Now stand feet together, legs straight…"

Eve obeyed, but her attention was on the muffled sounds of Han and Labren in the hallway. She strained her ears to no avail until the sounds disappeared.

"I demand an audience with Eve Ethan."

A loud voice broke through the hushed corridors on the first floor. Almost all of the children were romping outside, making the best use of the brief hour before dinner. Labren, resting in Professor Olof's office on his way to the dining room, lifted his head from a tome chronicling the genealogy of the Theodorics. If Ireic was set on offering him the crown, Labren intended to find an alternate possibility.

"You shall not speak to any one if you do not regulate your volume, sir." Han's voice carried despite the even tones.

"I will not quiet down until I get Eve."

Labren attempted to stand without the assistance of the desk. He managed, but pain sluiced through his thigh. A deep breath steadied him as he waited for the discomfort to settle to a dull ache. "Bring him in, Han," he called.

"Come this way," Han directed.

"I know Eve is here. They turned off at the crossroads and this is the first place on this road that has a wagon…." The man's voice trailed off upon setting his gaze on Labren. "You!" The man lunged forward.

Labren staggered back a step, his bad leg almost collapsing beneath him. He grabbed the back of the chair for balance.

Icy blue eyes spewed hatred. If Han hadn't kept his restraining hand on the man's compact shoulder, he would have seized Labren.

"Where is my sister?"

About hand's span shorter than Han, the man was built like a wall. Massive shoulders, solid chest, and well-muscled arms. His movements declared a skilled quickness on his feet and comfort in his own skin few men possessed. Labren scanned his face searching for a familial resemblance, but was hard pressed to find one beyond the blond hair and perhaps something about the set of his eyes.

"I demand to see my sister."

"You can demand all you want, sir, but you cannot assail this man."

"I have cause."

Han's eyebrows rose.

Labren frowned. "What cause would that be?"

"Kidnapping of my sister from her owner."

"I didn't kidnap her."

Approaching footfalls outside interrupted any further conversation. Not that they were really accomplishing much with the words they had exchanged thus far. Professor Olof appeared in the doorway, Eve at his heel.

Labren watched her face intently as she entered the room.

"I understand..." Professor Olof's voice was lost to the mutual cries of joy and relief from the siblings.

"Ruarc!"

Eve bypassed the Professor and ran into the stranger's out flung arms. The unfettered euphoria of her expression banished all doubt of the man's relation to her. Simultaneously, Labren's gut gave a terrible wrench. His knuckles whitened as his fingers dug into the upholstery. If only she became so overjoyed at his appearing.

"I thought I would never see you again." Ruarc stepped back, cradling her face between his hands. "I came to rescue you from Mridle only to find you gone, stolen away by some criminal, and dragged into harms' way." He pulled her into a massive hug. "Now put your mind at rest, little sister. I shall free you from this..." He uttered a word that Labren had only heard used by the roughest of the seadogs. Professor Olof's eyebrows rose and Han coughed. "He has no hold on you."

Eve tried to speak, but Ruarc shushed her. "Now, villain..." He turned and pinned Labren with a frigid glare. "Will you release her or do I need to call upon the law to deal with you."

Han stepped forward and opened his mouth, but Eve beat him to it.

"You don't understand."

"No, sister, you are the one who doesn't understand." Without dropping his glare from Labren, Ruarc pulled Eve behind him and pulled out a knife. "You are coming with me."

Balancing precariously, white fire searing his thigh, Labren raised both hands to hip level, showing the man his palms.

"She is not going anywhere," Professor Olof interjected.

"Would you attack an unarmed man?" Han asked.

"Remember what Father taught you. Listen!"

Ruarc ignored her, raising his knife slightly higher.

Eve ripped her hand from Ruarc's grasp. Frustration sparked green fire in her eyes. "Ruarc Ethan, you aren't listening."

Ruarc swung to face her. The mask of focused determination slipped and wariness flickered across his features. "Listening."

"I am free." Her voice weighed heavy in the room. "Look!" She pulled back the collar of her dress to reveal her bare collarbone. "He already freed me. I am his wife. It was my choice, Ruarc. I choose to stay."

A slow dawn spread across her brother's face. "So, he didn't steal you?"

"From Mridle's perspective, perhaps, he did. From mine, I was freed."

"But he is a criminal."

"Wrongly accused," Han pointed out before Labren's tongue formed a sound.

"The man from the caravan said he abused you."

"Let me guess his name," Eve offered, "Ulysses?"

"He was the one harassing her," Labren protested.

Ruarc glared at him. Distrust still hung between them. Labren didn't completely blame him.

Eve crossed to Labren and slipped an arm around his waist. "You are pale. Sit before you fall over," she whispered, guiding him back to the chair.

"But..." Ruarc's voice faded to silence.

Labren wanted to protest and remain standing, but a sudden wave of lightheadedness cut off the possibility. "What a way to feel useless," he muttered. "A brother-in-law I never knew I had threatens to abduct my wife and all I can do is struggle not to pass out at his feet."

"He becomes a bit intense at times."

"Intense?" The room shifted. Labren dropped his head between his knees, thankful for the gentle pressure of Eve's hand on his shoulder keeping him anchored to the floor.

"Perhaps Labren and Eve can explain everything at another time." Professor Olof suggested from the other side of the room. "We have refreshment and a room to rest in if you should need..."

"I am not leaving Eve with that man." Ruarc replied.

"I understand that. However, Labren needs her now."

"May I suggest a tray be brought here," Han suggested.

"Labren should be in bed," Professor Olof pointed out.

"What is wrong with the bloke anyway?"

"Recent injuries are affecting his health." Professor Olof pulled out a chair. "Will you please have a seat? I will gather something from the kitchen."

Ruarc settled in the seat, but Labren could still feel the steely pressure of his glare.

"Are there any other family members of yours I should know about?"

"No." Slender fingers slipped through his hair, lulling him toward sleep. "Our parents are dead, we only have each other."

It was a feeling Labren couldn't quite relate to. Ireic and he had never been particularly close, more from their parents' choices than theirs. It was hard to have a relationship of any kind while physically miles apart. Besides, the price on his head didn't help matters.

Chapter IV

Eve wanted to drop through the floor. Ruarc's glare burned the air between him and Labren.

Thankfully, Labren appeared oblivious of the intense emotions emanating from her brother. His fingers trembled. Her stroking his head seemed to relax him, but he needed to be lying down in his own bed. Since Ruarc refused to let her out of his sight, she scrambled for a compromise.

"Might we use the front room? There is a couch there for Labren."

"Perfect," Professor Olof said. "We will move him."

Han reappeared just in time to assist with trooping the whole party into the new room.

Ruarc continued to glower as Eve plumped pillows, unfolded and draped blankets, and then settled on the floor at Labren's side. Perspiration coated his face. She tentatively claimed the hand resting on the blanket. He weakly squeezed her fingers before closing his eyes and relaxing against the cushions.

Ruarc claimed the chair closest to Eve, and Han purposefully placed one immediately to his left. Only the professor remained standing. Pacing the rug for a moment, he allowed them all to drink in the tension before suddenly breaking it.

"Master Ruarc…" He raised an inquiring eyebrow.

"Ruarc Ethan, Seaman Ethan if you desire."

"Very well, do you mind if I call you Ruarc?"

Ruarc shrugged. "I have never been one to stand on formality."

"Eve hasn't volunteered much about her past so far. Perhaps you would be willing to enlighten us?"

"I don't know much more than her."

Han stepped. "She mentioned your father. Is he living?"

"If he was, we wouldn't be in this mess."

"Why?"

"Eve and I would be free citizens. She wouldn't be married to this…" Another slur. "And we would not be here."

Feeling sorry for Han, Eve decided to help. "Our father was a free man. Our mother was a slave woman owned by a friend. Father had partially purchased her from the friend when he died."

Her brother interrupted. "The bastard wouldn't honor the fact Father paid over eighty percent of the price upon his death. He claimed all three of us. He sold me within a month and I was at sea before the season changed."

Tears burned unbidden in her eyes. Eve blinked them back. "Mother died in childbirth that winter. He sold me to Mridle before her body grew cold."

Ruarc grunted. "I made him pay."

"So, you are still a slave?" Olof asked.

"Hardly. You don't see any collar here, do you?" Ruarc bared a naked neck. "I worked off my price a couple years back. I was just coming back for Eve." He pulled a leather bag from beneath his belt and dumped it on the table with a thunk. "That was to buy her freedom. A pretty hefty sum of gold considering she is of childbearing age and attractive." He eyed Labren. "Is there a chance that he would accept it and release her?"

"I told you. I have chosen to stay."

Ruarc studied her.

Eve met his gaze and tried to look as determined as she felt. Labren might not love her now or ever love her, but he was unerringly kind and considerate. Prince or criminal, she promised him before the Kurios that she would be his wife. Ruarc would just have to accept that.

Jaw set, blue eyes blazing, and barely restrained anger in every line of his face, her brother looked just as stubborn.

"Fine. But, I am not sure you are making a good choice." He swiped the pouch from the table and tucked it back under his belt.

Eve dropped her eyes to Labren's hand in hers. His long fingers were cold against hers, a sign that the fever was back. She watched him shift on the pillows, sweat glistening on his face.

The dinner tray arrived. In his movements, Olof crossed to claim Labren's other hand. His features immediately tightened.

"You are welcome to stay with us, Ruarc, until you are convinced. However, I am going to insist Labren be removed to his room."

"The fever is back?" Han moved to call for assistance.

"I am afraid so."

"I want to speak with Eve alone." Ruarc stood, confronting Professor Olof.

Olof studied him for a moment before shaking his head. "Trahern needs her and his health is more important than your right to answers. You will be given plenty of opportunity later, perhaps tomorrow."

Ruarc opened his mouth to protest, but the arrival of three large young men stalled him. Eve made efforts to making everything ready and ignored his efforts to catch her attention.

Early the next morning, Eve encountered her brother coming down the stairs when she was climbing up them. A laden breakfast tray filled her arms. Ruarc exploded.

"What are you doing? He expects you to wait on him, fetching this or that. You are no better than a slave, Eve. I heard that professor man last night. That man's health is more important to them than yours. They don't value you here. Come away with me and you will be truly free."

"No. You don't understand. I promised to care for him in sickness and in health."

Ruarc scoffed as he took the tray from her. "I think he is getting the better end of that deal." She led him up the remaining stairs.

"I promised." She opened the door to the bedroom. "Besides, he treats me like an equal."

Ruarc lifted the tray until it was even with her nose. "And this is a service that a common maid can render. Not the chore of a valued wife and equal."

"I do it because I care for him, Ruarc, not because I have to. You don't seem to understand that I want to do this. Now give it here. He isn't dressed yet and I don't want you disturbing him."

"Eve?" He caught her arm, suddenly serious. "You know I protest because I care. I am not leaving without you unless it is clear that you are being valued far higher than a servant."

"Ruarc, I am."

He frowned, but Eve didn't know how to convince him at that moment. Labren needed food and her own stomach was grousing. She left her brother standing in the empty hallway and slipped into the bedroom. *Kurios, please open his eyes. Let him see that I need to be here and do this.*

53

Despite the presence of Ruarc always lingering underfoot, Eve's life settled into a routine. She woke early, breakfasted with Labren, and then returned the tray to the kitchen on the way to her lessons. Ruarc sat in on every one, silently watching to be sure no one hurt her.

Labren appeared at lunch, assisted down the stairs by Han. Then the afternoon stretched into more lessons. Evening brought instrument practice, dancing instructions, and finally etiquette. By the time she finished her last lesson, dinner appeared in the dining room. Promptly afterwards, Labren needed assistance back to his room and Eve began her homework.

Labren's fever returned most nights. He alternated sweating and convulsing with cold. Each transition woke her because he pulled the covers on or off. Then the following morning, she began the whole regime again.

A month passed. Olof spoke of sending a letter to Prince Hiaronical to find out the state of the situation in the Anavrean court.

Labren opposed the idea because it would place his uncle in a tricky political position, knowing the whereabouts of an enemy of the state. He didn't want to place a strain on the already weakening ties between his father and uncle.

The argument took center place at each dinner. Olof built up a list of reasons for and Labren skillfully knocked each support down. Eve watched it all with a growing admiration for her husband's skill and knowledge. Her brother, on the other hand, watched in stormy silence that grew gradually calmer with each meal. By the end of a week, he took his place at the table and glanced at each opponent waiting with obvious interest to see who would attack first. Olof invariably opened the conversation. Before the main course appeared the debate reached full swing.

Eve woke after an unusually difficult night to find snow-like sleet icing the windows. She crept from the bed, dressed quickly before the fire, and slipped out without Labren stirring. When she returned with the tray, Labren opened his eyes.

"Thank you, Eve." He carefully lifted himself up so that he could lean back against the headboard. "I am not sure I am up for coming down for lunch today. I didn't sleep well last night."

"I know. You tossed and turned. Shouldn't the fever be

gone by now?"

"I would expect the same." He rubbed his face with the heels of his hands. "I will have to ask Olof when I see him this morning. How did you sleep?"

An urgent rapping at the door interrupted her reply.

"Professor Olof wishes to see you in his office, Eve," Han informed her when she opened the door. "I will see that Trahern eats his breakfast and take care of the tray. You better move along quickly. Olof is in a real tizzy about something your brother just told him."

"Do you know what it is about?"

"He mentioned something about patrols."

Catching her wrap from the end of the bed and throwing it around her shoulders, Eve hurried out the door. After a quick trot down the stairs and she reached the office door within a few minutes. Heartbeat thumping wildly in her chest and hunger gnawing in her stomach, she tapped on the ornately carved wood.

"Come."

Olof paced, eating up the carpet in long gangly strides. Ruarc stood to one side of the desk, arms crossed over his barrel chest, observing the older man.

"I told you it was foolish to think that they wouldn't find him. What is his crime anyway?"

"Ah, Eve, there you are. Please tell me how many patrols passed the caravan on a given day."

"One or two every week, sir."

"Different patrols? Composed of different men?"

"Yes."

"Were they wearing livery?"

"No, their clothes were what I expected of bounty hunters."

"Worse than I thought. How many to a patrol?"

"Six."

Olof shook his head. "It doesn't match the description. It must be someone else."

The front bell rang, echoing through the empty front hall. All three of them listened with forced calm. A moment later young feet approached the study door at a run.

"Soldiers in Anavrean royal livery at the door, Professor." The young man's eyes flickered from face to face. "Miz Abrigail would like to know when she should admit them."

Olof jumped forward, catching Eve's arm as he strode for the door. "You and Trahern need to hide now." He waved the boy out ahead of him. "Tell her to give us three minutes to clear the first floor and then stall them in the front room."

The lad nodded and disappeared back the way he had come.

"Ruarc go assist with the stalling." He ordered over his shoulder. "Most likely they are from the King and have tracked Trahern here." He paused as though realizing something. Dropping his grip on her forearm, he pinned her brother with a piercing gaze sharp enough to draw blood. "If you want your sister to make it through this day alive, you make sure those men don't reach the second floor until I return. Understood?"

"Yes." His jaw tightened and a hard glint flickered in his eyes.

Olof took the hall at a trot and the back servant stairs two at a time. Eve's heart hammered in her chest by the time they reached the second floor. Han and Labren waited for them outside the bedroom door. Labren leaned against the wall, his face tight. Han held a blanket roll under one arm.

Upon seeing them, Han immediately began running down a mental list in a hushed hurry, ticking them off on his fingers. "Their belongings are already stowed. The wagon and horses went to the farmer last week. All the students are already trained to withhold any details. You just need to give them the signal."

Olof nodded. "Good. I will." He turned to address Eve. Steely blue eyes bored into hers. "You and Trahern must hide now."

"Which room?" Labren asked.

"We are not going to be able to get you into the cellar, but Han put you in the supply room upstairs. I will go back down the way we came and stall them as long as possible. Han, come down to the offices as quickly and silently as you can. I will expect you there."

With those final instructions, he strode back toward the servants' stairs. Eve offered Labren a shoulder for support. He accepted it, shifting weight from the wall to her.

"All right," Han offered Labren a slight smile. "Don't make a sound and follow me."

Eve could hear Abrigail answering the front door in the

entranceway below. Any noise they might have made was covered by the sounds of stomping boots and the voices below.

The weight of Labren's body leaning on her reminded Eve of their trek in the woods. It seemed like ages ago to her. Yet, she knew only a few months passed.

Han reached the door to the stairs a few minutes before Eve and Labren. He waited as they carefully and steadily covered the short distance. Labren's leg was healing, but he had lost a lot of his strength. She strengthened her grip on his waist as they joined Han.

The climb up the stairs required more strength than Labren had. In the end, Han practically carried him to the top. Eve, carrying the blankets, followed them. After that, it was much easier. Han led them quickly across the large room that served as a recreation area and stage for the students. On the other side, he unlocked a small door.

He turned to Labren. "You know the rest." He laid the quilts on the floor inside. "I will lock the door and go down and see what is going on." Labren urged Eve inside, but placed a hand on Han's shoulder before he followed.

"Thank you, Atluer." Han gave him a quick embrace and then Labren hurried after Eve.

Before he shut the door, he smiled at them. "We will protect you." Then the door closed. Eve heard the lock click and the sound of the key being drawn out. Labren faced the door until Han's footsteps could no longer be heard.

Taking a deep breath, he turned and regarded her.

Labren's heart ached as he turned away from the door. He did not have much opportunity to dwell on it though. He was, at once, confronted by the frightened face of his young wife. Smiling to reassure her, he studied her face. Her green eyes, large with fear, overwhelmed her features. The ashen color of her skin made him wonder if she was going to faint on him.

"Come, we need to find the cupboard we are going to hide in." Hopefully, getting her mind on something practical would be distracting.

With great caution, they made their way through the maze of covered furniture, boxes, and trunks crowding the room. Sunlight poured in from the window on the west wall.

With only a few whispered instructions, they found the

cupboard that he remembered. A solid oak monolith, it stood against the wall farthest from the door. The body of the piece began a foot above the floor and rose to about Eve's shoulders. The length of the front was twice the height and four times the depth. On the outside it appeared to be just like any ordinary cupboard anyone would find in a pantry, kitchen or basement. When Labren opened the doors and lowered the false back, a gaping hole appeared. The space inside went back into the wall behind. A clever catch was installed into the trim around the false back so it could be opened from the inside or outside.

Eve shot him a questioning look when the false panel obeyed his fingers' command and revealed the small area beyond.

"Now would not be a good time to tell me you're claustrophobic," Labren joked.

Her horror answered his flippant remark. His insides clenched in dread as he watched fear tense the muscles in her hands, balling them against her skirt. She was going to panic on him if he did not do something. He pushed himself across the space between them. She fought him slightly when he first enclosed her in his arms, but then relaxed against his chest. He leaned against a nearby trunk, rubbing his hands up and down her back. They had to get inside, but how to tell her this.

"Do you trust me, Eve?"

The fair head bobbed slightly. Labren smiled.

"I trust you, too." His voice was soft. "Darling, we have to do this. You know that." He took a deep breath and smoothed her hair. "We can do this together, okay?" After a few moments, Eve finally nodded. He silently breathed a sigh of relief.

Deciding that she would probably feel less closed-in if she was closest to the door, he climbed in first. The area was too low to sit up in. Labren laid down full length and then slid sideways into the small space. Settling on the quilts spread on the rough wood, Labren finally motioned for Eve to come.

Her fear became tangible as she backed into the space toward him. Carefully, she latched the outer doors from the inside, and then she slid back farther so she could close the secret panel.

Labren felt her shudder as the latch caught with a soft click. "Labren?" Her voice broke.

"Yes."

"Where are you?"

Earlier Labren committed to not pursuing the physical side of their marriage during the day. He often ached to touch her hand or hair, but he held back. At night, he usually waited for her to fall asleep before he drew her close. She never protested and during the last few weeks her arms solaced him while the fever raged in his body. She comforted him when the shivers made it so he could not warm himself.

Yet again, Labren longed to reach out to her, but fear that touching her would nudge her over the edge into hysterics held him back. "I am right here." She rolled toward him and followed the sound of his voice with her fingers to his mouth.

"Hold me, please."

Not waiting for a second request, Labren reached out and pulled her to him. Her whole body shook as she buried her face against him. He whispered against her hair, "All you have to do is ask."

An hour later, Labren stared into the darkness and listened to Eve's steady breathing. Sleep brought her relief soon after they closed the door. Savoring the sweetness of her closeness, he breathed in the scent of her so that it filled his chest.

He cherished the tender sprouts of trust manifesting in the last weeks. Fear no longer darkened her eyes when the time came to retire. Ever since their last night with the wagon train, she had not resisted his embrace and closeness when they slept. In fact, more recently she had begun to curl up against his back at night. Thankful for the warmth her body gave, he also appreciated the effect of her presence on his sleep.

Since he was eight, death haunted his dreams. Each episode differed, but they all ended the same way: a lost fight to the death and a sudden awakening after the final blow. Heart pounding, sweat drenched, and nerves on fire, he frequently started up, gaining his feet before his thoughts. All that had suddenly changed on that night before they left the wagon train. No dreams came that night at all. Eve's sweet presence in his arms seemed to keep them away.

Eve shifted in his arms and nuzzled more closely to his chest. Labren moved to accommodate her new position. As he did, his hand fell to her shoulder. Warm, soft, and inviting, he fought his resolutions to not pursue her until she was ready. Gently he brushed his fingertips against the side of her face, closing his eyes to savor the silky softness of it. She sighed and turned her face toward his touch.

Thoughts of kissing her crowded his mind. As he did with increasing frequency of late, he wrestled them aside. He refused to rush her. He wanted her to want it too. Extra caution was a necessity because of the strength of the desire growing with each passing day. He groaned softly. There was no doubt in his mind that he wanted to go much farther than just lips to mouth.

Footsteps thundered distantly. Labren's heart jumped. He listened. The tempo and intensity indicated children. After a few moments, they pattered out of range.

What if it hadn't been just the children? The thought made his breakfast sour in his stomach. Death for them both would be the only answer. His father made it clear that Labren's life was worthless. Eve's would be even less valuable. The king wasn't one to wait patiently for nature to manifest whether or not she was with child. Hanging or simply the sword would deal with the problem.

His middle cramped. They had to escape notice. Eve must live.

Fingering the curling ends of Eve's braids where the pins were giving way, he wondered how it would look down around her shoulders. Only once, when she was drying it after washing, had he seen it in all of its golden waved glory. The scent of heather whispered to him. Someday, hopefully soon, he would be able to thread his fingers through the loose strands...

Pulling his thoughts up short, he tried to guide them back to the danger they faced. His plan of speaking with his brother and offering his services to the Secret Service as Labren Marcus no longer seemed plausible. Ireic intended to offer him the crown. Labren frowned. He didn't want it.

What kind of a king would he make? He hated bureaucracy and politics, much preferring straight answers and honesty. Formality and rank annoyed him. And, fashion was a joke. Well over half of the government was corrupt and self-glorying. Besides, Eve wouldn't fit among them. The thought of Eve putting on airs, spending hours on her toilet, or flirting with noblemen evoked a mixture of laughter and disgust. She would try to adapt. He knew she would, but he couldn't bear the thought of her trying. He loved her just the way she was.

He had never desired his birthright. Trained his whole life to claim it, he hoped to convince Ireic to keep it. Even with Ireic on the throne, his life with Eve wouldn't be completely untouched. Children would become a pressing necessity to secure the royal line and stability for the nation. He wasn't looking forward to that conversation with Eve. She still shied away from the topic or any possible reference.

She shifted slightly. A passing flutter of breath against his cheek made his heart thump wildly. No, Eve's needs and desires were quickly taking priority over anything else. She was his. She needed him. And, more importantly, he needed her.

"I need to shift my leg."

Eve jumped. Labren's arms tightened protectively around her. One hand caressed her shoulder in slow circles.

"Sorry, I did not mean to startle you."

Thoughts waded through the fog in her head as Eve struggled to remember where she was. The unique smell of her husband surrounded her. It felt too small to be the shack where they had stayed…she remembered. Thick walls closed in as the cottony air clogged her mouth.

"It's okay. We are safe." Labren's soothing voice met her rising panic. His lips brushed her ear as he spoke. "I am here," he reassured her. She clutched at his arms, but he evaded her hands.

"All I am doing is moving my leg into a better position."

His voice made it easy for her to follow his movements. Finally his arms returned to their places around her, but this time his face was even with hers. The warmth of his breath brushed her cheek. As though sensing her wariness, Labren asked, "Are you comfortable?"

"Yes," she croaked, barely above a whisper. Her mouth tasted disgusting. His hand in her hair and the warmth of his lips on her forehead distracted her from the gritty nastiness in her mouth for a moment.

"You seem less agitated." His chest vibrated beneath her palms.

"How long have we been in here?" She leaned into his warmth and wondered if his nightly fever was back.

"I would guess about five hours, give or take a half hour." He shifted his body weight again. In the process, his leg brushed hers. Suddenly aware of the stuffiness of their box, Eve's heart rate accelerated. She tried to fight the fear. She started whispering, "I am not going to panic," over and over under her breath. She concentrated so hard on not panicking that she did not realize something was wrong until something pressed across her mouth. At first she thought it was Labren's hand, but quickly realized it was not when he pulled her closer with both of his hands. He was kissing her.

Silently Labren prayed that she would not scream. Instead her lips yielded to his and she hesitantly relaxed against him. She tasted better than he had imagined. Her soft lips tempted him to deepen the kiss. Holding back, he chose instead to run his hand up her back and into her wonderful hair.

The sound of footsteps in the room outside brought his mind back to the danger at hand. He did not think it was Atluer out there. Maybe one of the children knew about this hiding place and told the men.

Reluctantly he relaxed his hold on Eve and drew his mouth away from hers. She let out a soft gasp and then fell silent. She trembled, but made no more sounds.

The catch on the cabinet's outer doors opened. He tightened his arms around Eve and prayed. *Father, Kurios, please spare us.* Heartbeats pounded in his ears as he strained to listen.

Thoughts scrambled about in his head. He had to save Eve. He had no hope if captured, but Eve might avoid death. If he could convince them that she was his mistress or a young girl he had brought to entertain him, maybe they would leave her here in the Professor's care. Of course they would watch her for a time to make sure she was not carrying his child. They would not know that there was no chance of that yet.

He strained his ears and waited to hear the lock on the panel releasing, but it did not move. Instead, someone tapped lightly on the wood.

"Han sent me up after a platter for Abrigail." The voice was muffled wood between them, but Labren recognized the voice of one of the students. The boy continued. "The messenger came ahead of the envoy with Prince Ireic. He came to give us time to prepare for the arrival of the prince and his company. Han will be bringing food up to you after everyone is settled for the night. I am going now."

Labren heard him scramble to his feet and close the cupboard doors. The muffled sounds of a box being moved and a squeaky hinge penetrated the wood. Finally the storage room's door banged shut.

"What about your leg?" Eve's concerned voice broke into his thoughts. "This immobilization is going to make it stiff. You need to exercise it every day in order to get the full use back."

"I guess it will have to wait. I will do those exercises that the Professor gave me when Atluer brings us the food."

Carefully, he stretched his good leg back behind him. Where was that back wall? His bones ached and he needed to move again. Eve rolled away from him as he shifted and did not roll back. Uncertain how to reach out to her verbally, he groggily settled into his new position. "I am going to try to sleep. Please wake me if you hear anything."

A barely audible positive response came from Eve's side of the box. Labren began to quiet his thoughts for sleep, but her state of mind bothered him.

Eve faced the wooden panel that separated them from the rest of the house. She pressed her palm hard against it to remind herself it was there, hidden from her eyes by the complete darkness. She was afraid of herself.

When she and Labren first met, she feared his death and worked to prevent it. Then once he regained consciousness, she worried he would force himself on her like the men that visited the tavern would have. Something about him made her trust him enough to marry him, though. Perhaps the lack of lust in his gaze or the respect and distance he gave her daily.

During the time since then, she learned to trust him completely. Right now, she never wanted to be separated from him again. Even hiding in a small hidden space in the attic of a school would not daunt her. Now, she realized, she wanted his touch. Eve pressed the wood harder. More than just being held at night and brief embraces during the day, she desired him. The question was did he feel the same about her.

A tear ran down her cheek before she could catch it. Surprised, she tried to catch the next one with her sleeve. The action reminded her of Sandra's rebuke that morning when she had tried to rub a spot off her face with the end of her sleeve. Apparently a noble woman would have used her lace handkerchief. That memory only brought to mind the many other times in the past weeks she had done something wrong. The tears flowed unchecked. Why would he want her? Once he had the crown, he would have his pick of the sophisticated women in the capital. Why would he want a commoner, a runaway slave?

"Eve?" Labren's voice was soft and hesitant.

She swiped at the moisture on her cheeks and did not respond.

He moved closer and laid a hand on her shoulder as he asked, "Are you all right?"

"I am fine," she said to the wall.

"No," Labren slipped his arm around her waist and moved so close her heart jumped. "You do not sound fine." As he brushed her hair away from her face, he caught a stray tear. "Oh, Eve."

He rolled her over to face him, his fingers brushing away her tears. "I am so sorry, Eve." Deep regret filled his voice as he held her tight. "I should not have kissed you like that. I broke my promise. You weren't ready. I should be shot for forcing myself on you. I promise it will never happen again unless you say. Do you believe me?" He surrounded her with his presence. "Please believe me, love," he pleaded. "Please, Eve, give me another chance. I need you. I would never hurt you." He buried his head in her neck and clung to her.

Cautiously Eve put her arms around him. He was so big and strong, yet he needed her. Eve could hardly believe it. She hesitantly touched his hair, barely brushing it with her fingertips. He did not move, not even to breathe. Slipping her hand into his thick hair, Eve finally whispered. "I love you."

Labren's head came up so fast it startled her. Swiftly he rolled her over and pinned her to the quilts, supporting his weight with his hands. "I wish I could see your face." He loomed over her. "Say it again. Please, Eve, say it again."

Not sure if he was angry or not, Eve timidly whispered, "I love you."

"Oh, Eve!" He sounded happy, but she was not sure yet. His next statement decided for her though. "I want to kiss you."

He paused as if asking for her consent, but she was too overwhelmed to speak. He wanted to kiss her again.

"Eve?"

She reached up and took his face in her hands and pulled it down to hers. His kiss was gentle, but sweet. When he drew back, she almost followed, but he prevented her. Afraid he was disappointed, she reached out to touch his face. A day's worth of scruff brushed her fingertips as he turned to kiss her palm. He moved over so that he was on his side and drew her close. She could feel his breath against her cheek. After a few moments he finally spoke.

"I love you, Eve." His voice trembled a little. "You are my precious wife." He kissed her and this time he did not pause.

Chapter V

A long time later, they heard the door unlock followed by footsteps. They both tensed.

"I think it is Atluer," Labren assured Eve.

After a few quiet shuffling sounds, the cupboard doors opened. The panel moved aside to reveal Atluer's worried features.

"Oh, good." He offered a hand to Eve as she scrambled toward him. "Turic said he had delivered the message, but you did not respond. I was concerned. The cubby is designed for one, not two. Olof insisted there would be air for two, but I..."

Eve gained her feet and immediately stepped away from the hole. Her hand shook as she reached for the back of the closest chair, but Labren could do nothing about it until he managed to get out himself. He told his leg to move, but it protested vehemently that it would not.

Atluer didn't bother waiting for him. Reaching in, he gripped Labren's forearm. Labren returned the grasp and they both worked to pull his reluctant body from the cupboard. His leg throbbed as he swung it out into the room. He eased his weight onto it only to have it give out.

"Whoa!" Atluer caught him as he sank toward the floor. "Eve, would you clear that chair?"

She folded back the dust covers for two of the chairs and a couch. Labren, with assistance, claimed the closest. Atluer began distributing steaming plates of food and pouring beverages from a laden tray. In the golden glow of an oil lamp and a dusty candelabra, the food looked delicious. The smells made his mouth water and his stomach growl. Labren shoveled a heaping forkful of stewed vegetables into his mouth and savored the tastes as they blossomed on his tongue.

"Your brother, Prince Ireic, is here," Atluer announced.

He handed Eve a steaming cup smelling strongly of peppermint. She set it on the floor.

"I know." Labren bit into a chicken leg, savoring the moist

texture despite the urge to satiate his starving stomach. "Turic told us."

Atluer set a mug at Labren's elbow. "What you don't know is that he wants to see you tonight."

Labren coughed, almost choking on his chicken. "Who told him I was here?"

Out of the corner of his eye, he noticed Eve lower her plate. She swallowed carefully without looking up.

"The Professor told him. I am to take you to see him as soon as you have finished eating. Are you okay, Eve?"

Labren turned his full attention to his wife. Her normally pale skin had taken on the shade of white porcelain. Setting down his plate, he reached for her. Atluer moved faster. He barely caught her falling plate as she slumped against the side of her chair.

Mentally cursing his leg, Labren got on his one knee and pulled himself to her side. "Do you have any cool water?" He asked Atluer.

Atluer shook his head and rescued the rest of the dishes. "I'll get the professor?"

Finding her pulse in her neck, Labren moved on to rub her wrists. "Is he in bed?"

"No," Atluer replied, as he cleared off a nearby couch. "He is downstairs waiting with Ireic in the back parlor."

Atluer lifted Eve from the chair and transferred her gently to the couch.

Frustrated at his inability to help, Labren pulled himself to his feet using a nearby trunk. He didn't like the way her head lolled back against Atluer's arm.

"If Ireic wants to see me tonight, he is going to have to come here. I am not leaving her."

"I understand." Atluer left, locking the door behind him.

Labren eased himself to the floor at her side. His hands swallowed up her cool fingers. He rubbed them gently. *Please, Kurios, let nothing be seriously wrong with her.* He stoked her cheek with his fingers. She was so pale she rivaled the dust covers' hues. Now that he was looking at her carefully, he realized she had lost weight since their arrival. Maybe she had not been eating lately. Racking his mind he tried to recall her eating habits of the last few days. He knew she ate, but he wasn't sure about the quantity. She worked so hard to take care of him, she probably neglected herself.

Labren smoothed back a stray hair from Eve's face. That was going to change. It didn't matter if his leg ached to the point of tears, she needed looking after too. "I am sorry," he whispered. He leaned over and gently kissed her smooth forehead.

His heart leapt when she stirred, turning her face toward him.

"Labren?" She sighed.

"Yes, Eve." He smiled as she opened her eyes and looked up at him. "I am here."

She slowly smiled back. "I dreamed that we were going to meet your brother." She shifted slightly.

Labren continued to stroke her cheek with the back of his fingers. He was just opening his mouth to explain that her dream was reality when Atluer returned with Professor Olof and Ireic behind him.

"She is awake," Atluer announced upon opening the door.

"Good." Olof waved Labren away so he could examine Eve. "This should only take a few minutes." He bent over her and began asking Eve questions in a lowered tone.

"Need a hand up?"

Labren met his brother's eyes across the offered hand. Ireic had grown a great deal over the five years since Labren last saw him. The slender young prankster was now a sturdily built, grown man. Accepting the help, Labren rose to his feet.

"Hello, Ireic."

"Hello, Trahern." Ireic smiled slightly and nodded a solemn greeting.

"Need a shoulder?" Atluer asked, appearing at Labren's side.

"Definitely." His thigh continued to throb and the muscles in the rest of his leg ached. Gripping the offered support, Labren let Atluer guide him toward the door.

Cloth-draped chairs clustered against the wall. Atluer left Labren leaning against a sturdy stack of trunks to uncover a few and Ireic assisted. Labren took the opportunity to study his half-brother.

Ireic's brown eyes bore a resemblance to his mother's and his solid frame hinted strongly of her side of the family. However, only these two features stood out as non-Theodoric. Labren did not remember his own mother. He had been told that she gave him the shape and color of his eyes and his natural grace. Yet, their father could have no doubt that these two men were his sons. They shared his dark coloring and hair. Labren found himself looking at a face similar to his own and wishing he knew his brother better.

Atluer returned to assist Labren to a chair.

Ireic, following Labren's slow progress, finally spoke. "Is the damage permanent?"

Labren could not see his face, but the tone of his voice indicated genuine concern.

"Olof says I will limp the rest of my life, but a cane is not inevitable. At the moment I am recovering from a secondary fever."

"And the lady?" Ireic took a seat across from him.

"Eve? She is my wife."

Ireic's eyebrows rose, but only for a moment. Labren couldn't help feeling encouraged. If Ireic accepted her, there would be hope for a familial relationship.

"I have come to offer you a pardon." Ireic looked down at his clasped hands. "Father is dying, though he refuses to acknowledge the fact. He ordered me on a progress along the border two weeks ago. I sought the council of his advisors and we decided I had best obey. Father has become volatile and even more mean-spirited these last few months. The nobles think he is feeling guilt; I believe he is frightened of death." He paused to swallow.

Labren sympathized with him, but his heart didn't stir at the news. *Kurios, give me wisdom.* Then reluctantly he added, *Please give my father peace and, if is Your will, knowledge of you.*

Pulling himself together, Ireic continued. "I have overwhelming public support and should have no trouble assuming power in the end. The country and the nobles want peace after all of the scandal."

Labren could understand that wish. A liege placing a price on his crown prince's head must have caused trouble among the nobles.

Ireic took a deep breath. "The problem is I don't want the throne." He looked up, meeting Labren's eyes. Fear and uncertainty lay barren for Labren to read. "That is the other reason I came to you. I was not trained to be a king, but you were. The crown was taken from you because of my mother's influence over our father. I do not believe you did anything wrong and many at court agree.

"If I endorse you, I doubt anyone would challenge your ascension."

Ireic's gaze pierced Labren to his heart. A strand of hope among the fear, the hope Ireic had pinned on his big brother coming to rescue him.

Labren turned his face away. This wasn't a surprise. Olof warned him. Of course, all the warnings and time in the world would not make this any easier.

"No." His voice came out more softly than he expected. He lifted his eyes to meet Ireic's. "I will tell you why.

"For years now, I have been an outlaw with an invisible brand on my name and face. I lost all my family ties both in Anavrea and here. I had nowhere I could go and be at peace, no one I could call friend. Even then, I served my country in disguise. I was a soldier and then a spy. Each time, when my past came to light, I was chased off with threats of physical harm.

"I was coming to you to seek a pardon, renounce my claim on the throne, and gain a chance at peace. Once gained, all I desired was a home for my wife and me. Then, I intended to keep in touch with you for the sole purpose of letting you know when the Theodoric line was secure.

"I cannot be at peace and be on the throne."

Atluer approached and interrupted. "I am sorry." He nodded apologetically to Prince Ireic before turning to Labren. "Olof wants to speak to you, Trahern."

"I don't think I should move much at the moment." Labren shifted his leg slightly and grimaced.

"Stay where you are," Olof instructed as he approached. Narrowly avoiding a trunk, he offered Ireic a half bow. Ireic acknowledged it with a nod.

"Eve is worn through. She is showing signs of extreme fatigue and lack of nourishment. The stress of the last couple of hours probably brought about the collapse." He regarded Labren with solemn eyes. "I also suspect she has not been getting adequate sleep. She will not tell me what the root problem is. I got nowhere when I tried to get a promise that she would relax. If she does not get some restful sleep soon, she is going to tumble into hysteria."

Labren nodded. "If you can provide us with a quiet room

and a bed, I will try my best to get her to sleep." He indicated the cupboard. "I can guarantee she will not get any restful sleep in there."

"She is claustrophobic?" Atluer asked.

Labren nodded.

"I don't see why they could not sleep in a normal room tonight." Ireic offered. "My men do not have to search the house again. If you can hide them in the servants' quarters, I see no reason they should be in danger."

"The men searched that part of the house this evening," Atluer agreed. "Abrigail and Stephen don't use the back most room and the servants' stair to the kitchen will be right outside in the hall."

With that settled, there was only the problem of getting them there with minimal sound. Labren watched Atluer return to Eve to explain the plan while Olof and Ireic discussed strategy. It was a short conversation. Afterwards, the professor left briefly to inform Abrigail of the change in plans.

Jealousy briefly reared its ugly head as Atluer leaned over his wife. Wrestling it down, Labren reminded himself of the past. He did not want to go through that again. Eve met his eyes over Atluer's shoulder and she smiled reassuringly. A warm sensation filled Labren's chest. In that one glance, Labren was reminded of her words and actions in that cramped little hole. She loved him and no one else.

They were not going to have to go back inside that little hole. The relief of that revelation drowned out all other thoughts. Eve missed the rest of what Han was saying to her. She looked up as he mentioned Trahern needing help down the back stairs. Following her thoughts, she sought Labren's face as he watched them from across the room. Their eyes met and she smiled.

He loved her. She still could not believe it. No one had ever loved her before. Well, no one she remembered except her brother.

"Eve?" Han's voice cut through her thoughts. "You have not heard a word I have said, have you."

Eve noted the hint of impatience in his voice as she drew her attention back to his serious face.

"Now, I know you are tired, but I need you to concentrate for a few minutes longer." He took her hand. "Do you think you could walk down stairs with only the professor's help?"

Eve nodded. "I am sorry, Han." She offered him a weary smile. "I will be fine with the professor's help. Are you going to help Labren alone?"

"I am going to ask Prince Ireic to help me with Trahern." He turned to rejoin the men, but looked back over his shoulder at her. "I would recommend calling Labren, Trahern while in Ireic's presence. That way you two can use Labren later as an alias." Eve nodded her understanding as Ireic approached.

"Ready to start?" he asked Han.

"Yes," Han answered. Turning to Eve, he introduced the prince. "Prince Ireic, I would like you to meet Eve Theodoric." Ireic smiled down at her warmly. He looked very much like Labren, only shorter and with different eyes. "Eve, this is His Highness, Crown Prince of Anavrea, Ireic Theodoric.

"It is a pleasure, Your Highness." Suddenly thankful for all the studying she had done since arriving at the school, she was about to rise and attempt a curtsey, but Ireic prevented her.

"Please don't get up, Mistress Theodoric. I am very honored to meet you." He paused as Han turned to the professor. Then lowering his voice, he said. "Please call me Ireic. We are sister and brother now." He winked. "I would be honored if you would consider me a friend. I do not have many I can trust, and I wish to add both you and Trahern to that list."

Olof approached and Ireic drew away to help Han. She rose to her feet and they were on their way.

With the professor's steady hand and guidance, the trip down to the second floor was uneventful for Eve. Abrigail was pulling the last wrinkles out of the bedding as they arrived.

"Ah, there you are. There is fresh water in the pitcher, and I changed the linens. Do you want some more to eat? Han said you didn't get much chance to eat."

Labren and his assistants arrived at that moment. All three men dripped sweat and Labren trembled from the effort, face pale as a ghost. He fell onto the bed with a groan and was still.

"You've gained weight since I last dragged you around." Han sagged against the door frame.

"Muscle," Labren replied. He rolled onto his side.

"Whatever it is, you are heavy."

"Thanks." Labren smirked before grimacing as he tried to

lift his leg from the floor to the mattress. Eve caught it and eased the foot the rest of the way. Not bothering with undressing him, she pulled the folded blanket at the end of the bed over him.

Abrigail pulled a heavy quilt from the chest beneath the window and handed it to Eve. "You two need your rest. Do you want food before you sleep?"

Eve met Labren's pained gaze and shook her head.

"Very well." Abrigail straightened her apron upon turning to Prince Ireic and Han. "Now, you two, out." She shooed the men out before her. She whispered to Eve as she closed the door. "I will bring you breakfast late in the morning. Sleep well."

The lock settled solidly into place.

"Eve?" Labren shifted. "Please come warm me, I can't stop shivering."

Eve crept over to the bed, covered him with the extra layer, and slipped in beside her feverish husband. She would be by his side no matter what happened. Even a crown would not drive her away. *Thank you, Kurios, for his love.*

Labren's breathing slowed into sleep about the time she settled her arms around him. Eve, more content and happy than she had ever been in her whole life, kissed his forehead and fell asleep listening to his steady heartbeat.

Labren savored the sweetness of Eve in his bed. Without opening his eyes, he lay still and listened to the rhythm of her breathing. Her solid warmth against his side radiated comfort. How had he ever thought he was complete without her?

The sun coming in the window above them warmed the small room. Its heat seeped through the quilts making his feet sweat. If he listened carefully, he could hear the sound of the children below eating the morning meal.

Slowly he opened his eyes.

Eve sighed softly and turned over, away from him. He prevented her from falling off the side of the bed. The movement roused her and the muscles in his legs. Pain sliced through his thigh, leaving a dull ache in its wake. Trying to ignore it, Labren concentrated on the beautiful green of Eve's sleepy eyes.

"Good morning." He smiled at her bewilderment. "We are waking late this morning." He drew her close and kissed her forehead.

"Where are we?" Her voice came out a husky alto, rough from sleep. "Oh, now I remember." With a smile, she snuggled closer. "How are you feeling?"

"I should probably be asking you that instead." He ran his hands through her hair. "You were the one that fainted last night."

He felt her smile slightly against his chest. "I feel fine so far."

"Good. Or else I would have to do something to my brother for putting you through so much last evening."

Eve shivered slightly at the memory.

Labren tightened his embrace and just soaked in the bliss he had been waiting so long for. She was his and he was hers in a way that he never thought he would be experiencing. She uttered a small sound of contentment and they fell back into sleep together.

Many hours later, after a cold breakfast and a short conversation with Abrigail, Eve and Labren pored over her history textbooks together. She was attempting to memorize the history of Anavrea.

"I hated this subject when I was here," Labren declared. Memories of reciting long chronicles to a younger Professor Olof in those far off days still made him flinch.

"But it helped you later, right?" Eve gently turned the page of the tome on the desk and smoothed the yellowing pages. "Especially the slavery laws. Are there Anavrean slavery laws that would affect my position there?" She looked curiously over at him.

Lying back on the bed, Labren regarded the peeling ceiling and tried to recall.

"The ways a slave can be made free in Anavrea are if the price the owner paid has been earned by the slave, the owner files the paperwork to free the slave, or the slave marries a free man or woman.

"Here in Braulyn, the owner has to free the slave or the marriage clause. Someone can buy the slave's freedom as your brother intended, but there is no way for a slave to earn his own freedom.

"Larkaria has very few slaves and those that are slaves have short enslavement periods.

"Sardmara is the worst, though. There you are a slave for life unless you can prove you were wrongfully enslaved." He frowned slightly. "The Sardmarians are the only active slavers in this part of the world. They have no laws about slaves having rights to decent living conditions and treatment."

He looked over at her.

"The Sardmarians are the only ones who sell their own people into slavery. All other slaves are indentured because of debt, or war." He grimaced. "Han was a Larkarian prisoner of war sold by his captors. He didn't know his parents or even his family name." He caught Eve's grieved look and tried to wipe the frown off his face.

"This is an awful subject to be discussing this early in the morning. I am eager for a change in topic." He grinned mischievously at her.

Eve set down the book and crossed to the bed. Leaning down to kiss him, she said, "Thank you for saving me from…"

She did not finish, because Labren had pulled her down on top of him and was intent on thoroughly kissing her. She was gasping for breath when they were interrupted be a light knocking on the door. Reluctantly, Labren drew back a little.

Preventing her from going very far, Labren called out. "Who is there?"

"Ruarc, I wish to speak with my sister."

Labren groaned, but Eve hushed him with a fingertip to his lips. "I will speak with him a moment and get him to leave."

She crossed to the door and opened it. Ruarc filled the opening and his anger rolled into the room in a tidal wave. "Han just told me you fainted last night. He is overworking you." He emphasized his point with a glare for Labren. "Look at him, lazy and good for nothing."

"Ruarc, now is not the time to discuss this." Eve moved to close the door, but Ruarc planted a foot in the way.

"No, now is the time. I want you to see reason before this ogre wears you into the ground. It won't stop until then. Just wait until you are with child. You will see."

The tone of Ruarc's voice drove Labren from the bed. He was finished with listening to his accusations without confronting some of them. Ignoring the pain that sliced through his leg, he pulled himself to his feet with the help of the bed post.

Eve, still unaware of Labren's movement, protested Ruarc's words in her own way. "Ruarc, you don't understand. You haven't been listening. I chose Labren. I chose this life. I have every intention of standing by my choice no matter what you say. I love Labren and he loves me." She looked up in surprise when Labren's hand finally rested on her shoulder.

"I don't appreciate you speaking to my wife in that tone, Ruarc."

Ruarc's chin rose in defiance. "You have no right to call her your..."

"Excuse me," Atluer's voice cut off Ruarc's vehement statement. "Trahern, your brother requests your presence in the study downstairs. I was sent to escort you." He looked from Ruarc's angry red features, Eve's pale cheeks, to Labren's tight jaw. "Is everything under control here?"

After a tense silence, Ruarc grunted. "Think about what I said, little sister. I speak the truth."

"You cannot speak the truth if you aren't willing to listen to it first," Eve whispered. She didn't meet her brother's eyes, but the line of her shoulders was defiant.

Ruarc turned away and stalked off in the direction of the bedrooms.

"Are you alright?" Labren asked, laying a hand on Eve's shoulder.

She nodded. Lifting her chin, she smiled weakly. "He will listen eventually." Her mouth quivered, but she steadied it. "Are you going to need my help with the stairs?"

"No." He smiled and stroked her cheek. "But I would like you to come with me."

"Of course."

Atluer stepped over to offer physical support. "Then let us head that way."

Eve knocked on the door to the study. They had taken the back stairs to the hallway by the schoolrooms. This smaller entrance to the professor's study was less obvious than the double doors that opened into the main hallway. Labren leaned heavily on Han's shoulders as they waited for the door to open.

Labren kept looking worriedly over his shoulder at the empty hallway. No one knew how long it was going to stay empty. Just as Eve thought she heard footsteps coming from the front hall, the door finally opened and Olof ushered them inside.

With Han's help, Labren made it to one of the chairs near the corner and out of sight from either door. Ireic perched on the desk facing away from them. Olof paced back and forth in front of Ireic. Han insisted she sit down before they did anything else.

"I don't want to have to catch you if you faint." He commented softly as she took her place. She shot him a mildly annoyed look and obeyed. She caught a wink from him before he retreated to the center of the room. Inwardly she smiled. As weird as it seemed, she liked that he was comfortable enough to tease her.

"A messenger arrived an hour ago with news from Ana City." Suddenly Olof advanced on Labren. "The King is dead."

Labren was used to the professor's abrupt ways, but Eve thought this seemed a little much. She grew concerned as Labren turn white.

"Olof!" Han leapt to Labren's side.

"That wasn't necessary," Ireic protested.

"You did not have to just jump him like that." Han was more upset than Eve had ever seen him before. He almost seemed angry.

Ireic turned to his brother. "I am sorry, Trahern." Pain and grief were written clearly across his features. "Eve?" Ireic turned almost timidly toward her. He was seeking forgiveness where none was needed. It was not his fault that the professor was showing no tact.

"It is not your fault." Labren spoke from behind her. "You and I knew this was coming." He rose as she turned to look at him. "I just did not expect it so soon." Ignoring Han's offered support, Labren looked to her. "Eve, take me back upstairs." His eyes were pleading and she could see the unshed tears threatening his defenses. He needed her right now. She walked over and offered her shoulders.

The men let them leave. Han spoke as they passed him. "If you need help, let me know."

Eve did not look up, but nodded as he opened the door for them. She was quite sure she could get Labren back to their small bedroom. What she could do after that, she was not certain.

About an hour later, Labren, exhausted and spent from grief, finally slept. Eve quietly slipped out the door and almost tripped over Han in the hallway outside.

"Is he okay?" Han asked the moment she had regained her balance. His concern touched her heart. Labren had a true friend in this man.

Smiling warmly up into his worried green eyes, she said, "He fell asleep a short while ago. The news hit him harder than he wants to admit."

Han nodded. He knew Labren well enough to expect as much. He treated both physical and mental pain the same way. "Is there anything I could do to help?" Han asked.

"You could wait here and listen for him," Eve replied. "I was going to go find the professor and, possibly, Ireic. I have some questions for both of them." She was uncertain what exactly she intended to ask, but she needed to understand the situation better.

"I will sit outside the door." As she turned to go, he offered. "I believe they are both up in the library. Ireic is taking the king's death pretty hard; so, don't be upset if he is short with you."

Eve turned back to look at him. She smiled. "Thanks. Don't block the doorway. Labren would not recover as easily as I did."

He acknowledged her gentle rebuke and settled into the chair a short distance from the door.

The familiar smell of dust and books greeted Eve as she passed through the large doorway into the school's library. She had spent many long hours poring over books of history, politics, and protocol in this room. The three floor-to-ceiling windows along the opposite wall looked out over the grounds spread behind the mansion. She knew the view well. One could watch the frolicking of the children on the lawn below or enjoy the majesty of the mountains towering against the sky to the west.

Ireic seemed to be doing that now. He stood in a classic pose, a dark shadow against the afternoon light. Shoulders squared, hands clasped behind his waist, and feet slightly apart, his stance suggested quiet and serious consideration. She doubted he contemplated the miniature young people moving about two stories below or the mountains beyond.

The professor was sitting unusually still. She found him watching her when she looked for him. He sat in an overstuffed winged chair between the two right most windows at Ireic's right. They were close enough to be in conversation, but Eve suspected a lengthy lull stretched before her entrance. Olof spoke softly to Ireic, "Eve is here," as she approached them.

Ireic turned. She stopped just beyond the end of the last table between her and the windows. His face was in shadow, but his body language spoke of hesitancy. Awkwardly, she waited for him to speak first.

"Princess Eve." His voice's steadiness contradicted his body's report.

She dropped into a small curtsy. Thankful that she had been practicing, she murmured a soft, "Your Majesty." He nodded as she rose.

"How is my brother?" Concern colored his voice.

"He sleeps, Your Majesty."

"Please." Ireic almost pleaded. "Don't be so formal. I want to put that off as long as I can." He stepped to the side and forward out of the light. She could distinguish the discomfort in his face as he continued. "Please call me Ireic or brother or…" He had run out of ideas. "…Anything but, 'Your Majesty.' Could you?" She slowly nodded. His face relaxed and he turned back toward the window.

"Do you think I will be able to convince Trahern to take the crown?" Eve followed him to the window.

"I do not know." She honestly did not. "I came to ask some questions of my own…Ireic."

He regarded her a moment and then smiled slightly. "I suppose you would have questions. Well, ask them. If I cannot answer to your satisfaction, I am sure that the professor would be able to." He swept a hand toward the strangely subdued man sitting in the shadows to their right.

She glanced at the floor. "What is my husband's standing legally?" She met Ireic's eyes. "Was he outlawed or just banished?"

"He was banished at first." The professor's voice answered from the shadows. "Then about a year later, he was outlawed in Anavrea."

Ireic agreed. "More recently Father issued a warrant for his capture, dead or alive. He offered a large reward to anyone who could deliver. That order changed Trahern from exile to fugitive even outside Anavrea." He sighed deeply. "My father feared Trahern or his offspring would challenge my line's claim to the

80

throne. I strongly disagreed with his actions and he knew it, but nothing would dissuade him."

"I understand." Eve spoke softly, but the prince's smile reassured her. "How can this be reversed?"

"It already has been. I sent my first royal decree back with the messenger that delivered the news of the king's death and my ascension. Trahern has been granted a full pardon. The main problem now is whether or not he is to be reestablished into the Theodoric line as an heir."

The professor stood and addressed them both. "We should wait until Trahern is with us to discuss this." Eve had been thinking the same thing. "He, no doubt, has some questions of his own for both of you."

Eve's head came up as Ireic turned toward the door. "Why me?"

"You are his wife." The professor stated it in such a way that Eve felt he thought it should be obvious that she would have a say. "If he becomes king, you will be his queen." She was not sure she felt comfortable with that thought no matter how often she was told. She was only a common slave, hardly royal material.

Olof smiled at her puzzled face. Laying a hand gently on her shoulder, he said, "Eve, you are no longer a possession that is taken and sent as her master sees fit. You must stop thinking like a slave. I know Trahern does not want you to regard yourself that way. Does he?"

Eve remembered the conversation she and Labren had shared over a breakfast campfire. He wanted to treat her like a wife. "No." She looked up into the wizened eyes of her teacher. "But it is so hard to change something that has been a part of me for so long. It was beaten and starved into me from before I can remember." She carefully reburied the memories that rose. Labren changed her life for the good. He needed her now and she must not fail him.

"I will go fetch him." She started for the door, but Ireic caught her elbow gently.

"Can I come?" His dark eyes had a numb, empty look to them. Like the man behind hid from something too terrible to confront. Something was familiar about the look.

She shyly dropped her eyes and turned.

"Where should we meet you, Professor?" Ireic did not

release her arm.

"In the back parlor would be best." The elder man replied. "Is half an hour long enough?"

They consented and quickly left. The professor watched them negotiate the large door together. Ireic had to move quickly to get to the door ahead of her. He made a point to open the large oak panel for her to walk out into the hall. Swiftly, though, he somehow caught her elbow again before she had gone three steps past the doorsill.

They moved in silence to the stairwell, but as she took hold of the railing, Ireic stopped her.

"Han spoke of your most recent confrontation with your brother."

Heat rose to her cheeks despite the knowledge that her brother was the one who should be ashamed.

"I wish to help. Would my speaking to him assist you?"

She shook her head. "I doubt it. He is convinced that Trahern is abusing me and treating me like a slave not a wife. I have told him repeatedly that it is not the truth, but he will not listen. He refuses to let go of an idea once he is convinced of it."

"I know the type. Then it would be better to have him distracted by something more pressing."

"But what?"

He smiled. "That is one advantage of being king. I will find something."

"Thank you."

"You are very welcome, sister. Come, let us check on Trahern."

Chapter VI

Two days later in the late afternoon, Eve went searching for the brothers. As she pushed the heavy oak door into the library, she wondered how their plans were coming. As far as she last knew, she and Labren were leaving for Ana City with Ireic on the morrow. Labren hadn't specified how long they were going to be staying in the capital or what he wanted them to take. The view that presented itself to her as she entered the room drove all thoughts of packing to the back of her mind.

The dignified uncrowned king of Anavrea was in his elder brother's headlock. Both men had abandoned their jackets and Ireic's hair stood on end. She spotted the missing clothing on a nearby table, but did not see Labren's cane among the cloth. Their laughter quickly dispelled any possibilities of serious strife.

Labren addressed his brother as she approached. "I see I should have stuck around to teach you how to fight."

"I know how to fight," Ireic managed as he tried to get a good grip on Labren's forearm. "I just never learned how to wrestle." With that, he went suddenly limp. The abrupt change from struggling to dead weight caught Labren off balance and they both went down laughing, narrowly missing the table behind them. Eve rushed forward to help them to their feet, only to be caught by Labren and pulled down with them.

"Have you come to make me behave?" Her husband's voice came from behind her left ear. She struggled against his firm grip on her waist.

"No." She finally succeeded in slipping his grasp. She gracefully arose and smiled down at him from a safe distance. "I have given up on that."

Ireic had managed to gain his feet also and offered Labren his hand. "I suggest you rise, Trahern. She is more dangerous than she looks." He shot her a familiar wink.

Taking the hand, Labren pulled himself up onto his good leg. Eve noted his cane was sitting against a desk a few feet away. He had obviously not been following orders. Her brief lapse in focus gave him the chance to cross the distance between them. She turned back to them only to encounter the wall of his chest and his blue-eyed gaze from over her head.

"My wife and brother seem to be getting along well."

Eve did not look up, but continued to stare at the buttons of his new shirt. She had chosen the blue material because it complemented his eyes so well.

Labren knew she had heard him. Dropping his voice to a level that Ireic could not hear, he said it again. "My wife and brother seem to be getting along well. Maybe he should be the one to break the news."

"Playing the coward, Trahern?" Both Eve and Labren jumped at Ireic's closeness.

"Yes." Labren looked over at his brother.

"In that case." Ireic looked amused and uncomfortable at the same time. "Trahern warned me that you were not going to be pleased with my plans." Labren turned to follow Ireic as he approached a nearby desk. "I wanted both of you to come with me back to the capital. I still strongly believe that Trahern is the man who should be on the throne and not me." Ireic slid a pile of papers off the desk. "As you already know Trahern disagrees with me very strongly, but we have reached a compromise." He perched on the edge of the desk and faced her.

Labren had moved to her side. Expecting that he would touch her in some way, Eve was surprised when he did not. Ireic continued.

"Labren has agreed to return with me to Ana City for a few months."

Labren broke in. "Two months."

"Yes, two months," Ireic agreed. "During this time he will be helping me to set up the new regime. At the end of that time, I will no longer have any claim on his time. The two of you will be free to disappear, withdraw into the country, or whatever you wish."

"You are leaving out some important issues." Labren's voice came from behind her left shoulder. He was standing closer than she had originally thought. Ireic raised his eyes from hers to her husband's.

"I want Trahern to be reinstated into the line to the throne." Ireic continued without lowering his gaze to hers. "Then, if I die before you have children, he becomes king. Your first child would become heir the moment he or she is born." He dropped his eyes to Eve's. "If I die before the child reaches the age of majority, Labren would serve as regent for the remaining years between."

Eve's mind raced. "Would the child remain with us until the age of majority?"

"We will teach and raise the child as we see fit." Labren answered. "Ireic and those in government will have no say in his or her training."

Eve took a step toward Ireic as he perched on the end of the desk. "Have you completely ruled out marriage and children for yourself?"

The Prince's head came up quickly and surprise spread across his face.

"Trahern asked me the same thing." He pushed off from the edge and strode into the middle of the room. "All I am doing is trying to secure the throne in the event I die or never produce an heir. I plan on choosing whom I marry on the basis of other things than birthing ability. Unlike my father, I want to have a mutually enjoyable union." He turned back to them. "Like you."

Eve smiled and almost laughed. Labren stared intently at the carpet, but when Eve glanced at him his shoulders were shaking slightly. "Although I am sure Trahern would agree with you, we are not a good example of a marriage that started on love or even affection."

Labren slipped an arm around her waist. "But I, for one, am flattered that you approve of our relationship." Laughter still lingered in his voice, but Labren tightened his embrace to emphasize his seriousness.

Eve turned and planted a kiss on his cheek. "I need to return to packing."

She was halfway to the door when Ireic protested. "You have not given your answer."

She turned. "Where Trahern goes, I go." After curtseying slightly, she left the library.

An hour later she looked up from placing the last of her new clothes in the last trunk to find Ruarc watching her from the bedroom doorway. Bracing herself for the coming fight, she prayed for strength and wisdom.

85

"Have you come to say goodbye?"

Her brother frowned. "I have. I leave tomorrow morning for Ratharia."

Eve stared at her brother in shock. Ireic promised to give her brother a task, but sending him to Ratharia seemed extreme.

"It isn't that bad, Eve. I have been there dozens of times. King Ireic needs a man who knows the culture to find out what his ambassador is up to. Apparently the reports have been sketchy and unhelpful."

"How long will you be gone?"

He shrugged. "Unknown." His eyes narrowed. "You really do love him, don't you."

"I told you."

"I know."

"What made you finally listen?"

He frowned. "Your new brother-in-law can be mighty persuasive."

"What did he threaten?"

"A cell in his dungeon if I didn't stop harassing his sister-in-law."

A drastic tactic but if the threat worked Eve was content. "So you believe he loves me now?"

"No. But I do believe the king will not let him abuse you."

It wasn't what she wanted, but it was a beginning.

"You could come with me if you wish, Eve."

His desire for her company tore at her heart, but she knew where she belonged. "No, Ruarc. I have found where I belong. It is with Labren." She closed the trunk lid.

He turned to leave.

"I will miss you, Ruarc."

He turned back. "Even with him."

"He isn't my brother."

He crossed the room. Enveloping her in a bone crushing hug, he whispered, "I love you, Eve." Then he left.

Eve sat on the trunk and struggled with the turmoil within her chest.

After an afternoon and evening of frenzied packing and preparing, they set out for Ana City early the next morning. This journey passed differently than the previous. They traveled with twenty armed men to protect them. Secondly, Ireic, Olof, Han, Labren, and she all traveled in a carriage for the first day, making for close quarters. Eve got sick halfway through the day. She spent the rest of the week on the road feeling weak and could barely eat. The professor insisted that she drink a strong tea with every meal, but she did not improve.

She missed the privacy she and Labren shared back at the school. In the traveling party, they never gained a moment to themselves. Even at night, they all slept close to the fire. When they did stay in an inn one night, Labren stayed down with the men discussing important details until she fell asleep from exhaustion. When he finally did come to bed, she could only snuggle close and fall back to sleep.

Then, the night before they were to reach their destination, Eve surprised all of them, as well as herself, by bursting into tears over a spilled cup of tea. Feeling ashamed of her weakness, she fled to the carriage and hid inside. She was hungry, but she was not hungry enough to face a group of men with her eyes red from crying. Pressing her face against the brocade upholstery in the dark coach, she let herself cry.

As Eve fled, Labren felt like someone drove a knife into his chest and twisted it. He dropped his head into his hands. How could he have been so blind? He was committing the mistake he had been trying so hard to avoid. Someone laid a hand on his shoulder and asked, "Are you all right?" Instinctively, he nodded. He was not in physical pain, just emotional. He had neglected the one person he loved more than anything else in the world, all because he did not want to be forced to neglect her for the rest of their lives.

Fixing a passive mask on his face, he raised his head. Atluer was squatting next to him with a hand on his shoulder. Understanding and concern filled his eyes.

"Where did she go?" Labren heard his voice coming out like a growl.

Atluer peered at him a moment before answering.

"She headed in the direction of the carriage," he finally answered. "Be gentle with her." Nodding, Labren grabbed his cane and started in that direction as fast as his leg allowed.

He spotted her the moment he looked through the carriage

window. Quietly he opened the door. She did not stir as he pulled himself up onto the seat across from her. Pulling the door closed behind him, he looked over at her small form. Strands of hair fell over her arms in waves of gold. Knees drawn to her chest, she rested her head on them. She gave no indication that she knew he had entered the compartment. He waited, not sure what to do.

"I am sorry." Her tearful voice cut through his thoughts.

"There is nothing for you to be sorry for."

She slowly raised her head to look at him. The pain, fear and confusion in her eyes pulled at his heart. Her bottom lip trembled and he could not stay away. Crossing to her, he took her into his arms. He held her close and buried his face in her hair, willing his heart to stop hurting. After a moment, he felt a movement near his heart. A few moments later, she spoke.

"Your heart is racing." Her voice caught.

"I am frightened." Labren loved the way she fit in his arms.

She pushed away from him so she could see his face in the dim moonlight.

"Of what?" The shadows did not hide the concern in her eyes.

"I have been neglecting you. I am afraid because, I cannot promise that it will not happen again. In fact, I know the next two months are going to be hard." He stopped because she had placed her fingers on his lips.

Looking straight into his eyes she said, "I love you."

"I know, and. . . ." She stopped him again.

"That means I will gladly go where you need me." He stopped her.

"It does not mean I should neglect you. I promise that in two months I am all yours. Can you survive that long?" Labren's heart strained with each beat. She had to say yes.

Eve studied his face. "Do you love me?"

Without hesitation, he answered. "Yes!"

"Then I can survive."

With those words, Labren mentally sighed with relief. He pulled her close and kissed her thoroughly. When they finally drew apart, Labren suggested, "We can sleep in here for tonight."

Eve agreed.

Labren left briefly to gather their bedding and by the time he returned, Eve had picked a place for them on the upholstered benches.

Eve's lungs labored for each breath. Through sheer will power, she kept the claustrophobia at bay. The two small windows on either side of the carriage supplied inadequate circulation. Part of the problem was her cramped position. Although she and Olof were the two smallest people in the group, they were not the most comfortable.

The carriage continued its swaying way along the dirt road. Eve tried to adjust herself. Then they hit a bump.

"Oomph." Labren grunted as her elbow connected with his ribs.

"Sorry," Eve whispered. Instead of complaining, Labren slipped his arm around her and pulled her back against him.

Leaning over slightly so that his mouth was next to her ear, he said, "Hold still."

Catching her breath and biting her bottom lip, Eve tried to comply. Her muscles screamed that she move, and her stomach issued its usual threats. She was crowded, nauseous, and bone weary.

The carriage maker intended the vehicle for three to four people. The designer would have been shocked to see three rather large young men, an older gentleman, and a small woman packed into the main compartment. On any other day, one or two of the men would have ridden on one of the fine horses tethered to the rear of the wagon, but today they were going to reach Ana City. The king or those in his intimate circle of friends would be looked down upon if they rode into the city like a common soldier. For appearance, they suffered together.

Eve squished between Labren and the professor in the seat facing the front of the contraption. Ireic and Han squeezed into the seat facing them. A tangle of knees and feet obscured the floor.

Claustrophobia pulled the four walls close. About the time she thought she could not stand it anymore, the driver called out from above.

"Ana City!"

Raising her eyes in hope to the window and the free, open space passing beyond it, Eve longed for the end.

"I understand how you feel." Ireic said from his seat, knee to knee with Labren. He caught her attention with his warm brown gaze. Fine lines etched around his eyes and fatigue painted his cheeks pale. "I would prefer anything to this."

"I wish we had our wagon again." A wheel jumped out and then back into a rut making Eve bite her tongue. "At least we had space."

"It is almost over," Han pointed out with a wan smile. "Just remember. We won't have to listen to anyone's snoring tonight." All of them looked toward the snoozing professor.

Labren laughed softly. "I believe he frightened every beast for a couple miles every night." The arm around Eve's waist tightened slightly. "I, for one, am looking forward to a hot bath and a soft bed." Both Han and Ireic murmured their agreement to this.

The carriage wheels struck the edge of the pavement with a jarring thump and then glided along more smoothly than they had in days. Silence again descended and Eve turned her attention back to the distant window and the forbidden freedom beyond.

A few moments later, they heard cries of greeting from a chorus of male voices. The hollow sound of a drawbridge echoed beneath the wheels.

"The gates," Ireic informed them dully.

His statement must have been true because almost immediately the horses slowed and a voice inquired, "What is your business inside the city?"

"King Ireic's personal business," the captain of the escort replied, tapping the crest on the carriage door. "Let us pass."

"By all means."

The sound of moving men and horses precluded an abrupt start. Outside the window, Eve glimpsed immense, wooden doors and the bottom of a portcullis. The rattling of cobblestones under the wheels began. As the sounds of everyday peasant life drifted in to the crowded passengers, all three men listened with memory-hooded eyes.

Eve was reminded of the world that she had left behind in Braulyn. So much had changed since then. Now she was loved, something she had never expected. She also had friends, Eve realized as she looked across at the three other men in the carriage. This revelation gave her a secure feeling. She was no longer alone.

The journey through the city streets took longer than Eve expected. It was at least a half hour after they passed beyond the gates before they finally ground to a halt and the door closest the professor and Han opened.

Stiffly, the professor unfolded himself and climbed out. Han and Ireic followed. Hesitant and suddenly nervous, Eve accepted the gloved hand offered and ducked through the door into the dimming afternoon sunlight.

After the momentary blindness passed, Eve realized that a large group of people were standing before her. She heard the carriage groan. Labren stepped to the ground behind her with a sharp intake of air. His leg was probably bothering him again. She turned to look up into his bent face.

"Are you all right?" she asked.

Labren nodded slowly before opening his eyes. "It does not like being moved after it has been sitting for a while." He managed a weak smile. "I will need your shoulders though." Their actions, smooth from repeated maneuvers like this, brought Labren forward, straight and tall with his right arm around Eve's shoulders for support. This way she could support his body weight if his leg gave out or the pain became unbearable.

Now Eve got a good look at the group waiting to greet them and her heart sank. Most of the men were dressed in elegant clothing covered by identical dark brown robes. Standing a little apart from these men was a smaller group of many ages, sizes, and wearing different degrees of attire. Except for one woman, their clothing seemed to be the kind a high ranking servant would wear. The exception was a sophisticated young woman of about Eve's age. She wore a more regal looking costume than the others and carried herself with somber dignity as if that was all she had left.

"My sister," Labren informed her as they stepped forward to be greeted. Racking her brain, Eve tried to remember if either brother had told her about a sister. "Don't look so startled, Eve." Labren's voice was low enough for only her to hear. "I will explain later. Just look composed and self-assured. Ireic and I will take care of everything." He tightened his grip on her shoulders and Eve tried to relax.

"Welcome home, Your Majesty." A tall thin man stepped forward from the group of men. A heavy silver chain hung around his neck that his comrades lacked. It fell forward as he bowed deeply and gracefully.

"It is good to be home." Ireic nodded his recognition of the councilmen and then turned to the smaller group of servants.

"What? No greeting for your older brothers?" He asked the elegant woman Eve noticed earlier.

An almost completely hidden flicker of surprise passed over the girl's face before she stepped forward.

"Of course," she replied, curtsying daintily. "I am just overwhelmed at the shock of seeing both my brothers home at last." She dipped her head remorsefully. "Pardon my lack of decorum, dear brothers."

"Granted," Ireic replied. His movements were calculated and measured. His face showed none of the emotion Eve would have expected at the reuniting of siblings after their father's death.

What followed these initial greetings Eve could only describe as a dance. Each dancer knew the complicated pattern to be executed. This hand there, that foot here, bow to the King, dip for the councilmen, each player knew their part and preformed it perfectly, scorning those who had not.

Eve did not understand the strategies and none of her training at the school prepared her for the elegance and cruelty of these proud dancers. She forgot that she was to nod at the councilman and almost dipped, giving them more esteem than due. Thankfully Labren caught her mistake before the others noticed. After the near miss, he whispered and coached her through the maze of people. His effortless negotiations were so smooth, she was shocked with all the others when he stepped out of sync and stopped the dance.

"Princess Eve will not be residing in the Opal suite." Labren's voice was calm, but Eve could feel the hard determination beneath the placid tones. A slight echo reverberated in the silence as all, two servants, the head butler, the councilor with the silver chain, and, of course, Ireic, stopped moving and talking. Ireic and the councilor turned to regard Labren.

The councilor spoke first. "Which suite would you prefer her to reside in?"

"She will be residing where I reside, which, I believe, is where I quartered before I left." His placid tones disguised an undercurrent of pain.

The councilman turned white and an expression of mild admiration passed across Ireic's face. For a moment the mask was gone. A smile played at his lips and laughter glinted in his eyes.

The councilman spoke. "Tradition mandates that each

member of the royal family has their own quarters."

"Do you and your wife keep separate quarters?" Labren's voice challenged the older man's superior smirk.

"As a matter of fact we do." The man was obviously proud of their practice.

"I feel sorry for you." Labren's face showed genuine sympathy, but Ireic struggled not to laugh. One of the maids coughed and the butler frowned carefully, but Eve gained the impression that he wanted to chuckle.

Quickly pulling the mask back on, Ireic finally spoke to the now red-faced council member. "Very well, Princess Eve and Prince Trahern will be residing in the north wing. There is more room there than the old quarters. Of course if you would rather…?" Ireic raised an eyebrow as he regarded his brother.

"That would be wonderful, dear brother." Labren replied immediately. "Those rooms have direct access to the gardens, a beautiful place for my young wife."

"Now, if there is no new business?" Ireic addressed the painfully still man at his side. The councilman managed a weak head shake to indicate there was none. "I will retire to my rooms. It has been a long day." Ireic quickly bowed to Labren, Eve, and nodded to the councilman. Turning on his heel, the king quit the hall in the direction of the royal quarters.

"We will also leave." Labren announced. "This way, my dear." They left the room without acknowledging the councilman, but Labren pointedly nodded to the stunned butler and two servants.

Later in their rooms, Labren visibly relaxed in his chair the moment the door closed behind the last servant.

"I forgot how awful this whole life is." He sighed loudly. "If I had remembered, Ireic would have never talked me into this crazy idea." Wearily he rested his head on the back of the chair and closed his eyes.

Without the life in his eyes and their distracting glimmer, the strain of the past week of travel was plain. Slightly blue circles ringed his eyes and fatigue pulled at his mouth.

Kurios, please give him strength. Eve crossed the room to kneel next to his chair. Taking his right boot into her lap, she began to work on the lacings.

"You promised Ireic two months, correct?" She glanced up to find her husband watching her hands work.

"Yes, but with the way things look, he is going to want me longer." A small fearful flicker gripped Eve's heart. She was about to ask for an explanation when someone knocked on the door. As she rose to get it she tried to convince herself that Labren would not agree to stay longer, but she failed. He loved his brother and his county.

As Eve approached the hall door, she heard the sound of a child's voice on the other side. Puzzled, she was even more surprised to find Ireic when she opened it. The young woman introduced as his sister accompanied him and holding her hand was a young girl child of about two years.

"Uncle?" The toddler regarded Eve with liquid, dark brown eyes.

"No, Isica," the young woman corrected. "Aunt."

"May we come in, Eve?" Ireic asked. "I promise we will not linger long."

Stepping aside, Eve let them pass. "He is exhausted," she warned Ireic.

He flashed a reassuring smile before disappearing into the living area where Labren sat. His sister followed with the child in tow. Eve carefully closed the door.

"Ah, Trahern," Ireic stepped forward.

As Labren started to rise, Eve rushed forward to protest.

"Your leg is swollen." Pushing him gently back into the chair, Eve further prevented his movement by taking his foot again into her lap and continuing work on the laces.

"Sorry," Labren managed through gritted teeth as Eve shifted the foot. "It seems I am not going anywhere."

"That is fine." Ireic took a seat on a couch opposite his brother and gestured to the woman and child to join him. "Yulandra wanted to see you as soon as possible and I was worried about your leg."

"Isica." The young woman, Eve deduced was Yulandra, spoke to the child. "This is your Uncle Trahern. I told you about him. Do you remember?"

Regarding Trahern with large eyes, the girl stuck her finger in her mouth and pointed at Eve with her other hand.

"Who she?"

"I believe she is your aunt…"

"My name is Eve." Eve smiled and Isica smiled back. "Would you like to come over and play in the garden some day?" To Eve's delight the child looked interested and turned a questioning face toward her mother. Yulandra nodded her approval and shot Eve a friendly glance over the girl's head.

"We both would be delighted."

The fear and hesitancy vanished in the young woman's face and Eve felt she could hope she found a friend as well as a sister. Two things she never had before.

Sensing Labren's pain, Ireic decided it was time they left him to rest and said as much.

"Do not worry about starting tomorrow, Trahern." The king paused before following the females out the door. "I think I can handle it for a day and you need your rest."

"Thank you." Eve whispered after her brother-in-law. "He needs it."

Ireic nodded knowingly before disappearing down the hall. Eve was sure she caught a worried look in his eye. Regardless, she had a husband to put to bed.

A few months later, Eve awoke to the delicious weight of her husband's arm lying across her stomach. It was a rare and welcome sensation. She tried to linger and savor it. The sweet sound of Labren's breath, the pleasant warmth of the bedclothes, and soft breeze blowing across her face were all wonderful invasions of the senses, but other sensations encroached. They elbowed their way to the forefront. A thick throbbing began at her temples and her stomach revolted.

Her middle had been doing this every morning for almost a week now. Most mornings, when it woke her, Eve obediently stumbled to the bathroom and emptied her stomach, but this morning was different.

Labren had not hurried off to his duties before she had awoken. Breaking from his habit of being up, dressed and gone by the time her stomach forced her to the chamber pot. For months, she had barely seen him and since he had not run off yet today, Eve was determined to linger in his embrace and her middle was just going to have to wait.

That was the plan. Eve found it more difficult by the

moment to lie peacefully enjoying her husband's presence. In fact, within five minutes of deciding not to let her stomach have its way, she dove desperately toward the bathing room. She made the move so abruptly that Labren went from contented, oblivious sleeper to worried husband almost instantly.

"Eve?" His sleep-ragged voice followed her to the tiled room. "Are you all right?"

The sounds of retching answered him which brought him immediately to his feet. By the time Eve's stomach tried to climb her throat the second time he was there. Brushing and holding her hair out of the way, he silently rubbed her back to soothe her.

When she finally finished and he returned from emptying the pot, he scooped her off the floor. "You should not be on the cold tiles." He carried her back to the bed. Setting her down and sprawling beside her, he looked over and asked, "How long has this been going on?"

Eve avoided his eyes. "About a week."

"Eve, please look at me."

She did.

"Do you have a stomachache? A fever?" His blue eyes clouded with worry as he reached to feel her forehead. "I do not think you should be entertaining Yulandra today. You should rest."

Eve instantly opened her mouth to protest, but was interrupted by a noise coming from the front of their quarters. Now, after growing accustomed to living in the palace, Eve was finally confident that the sound would be dealt with. Their servants learned, after the second week, that neither their master nor mistress needed assistance with dressing and a myriad of other things Eve did not even know you could be assisted with. Now the servants only cleaned, served meals, answered the door and announced visitors.

A moment after they heard a burst of cheerful, childish chatter, a maidservant appeared at the bedroom doorway. "Her majesty Princess Yulandra and her daughter are here to visit Princess Eve."

"Thank you, Lisip." Eve shot Labren a defiant look. "Please tell her I will be right out."

"Yes, Your Hi…Madam." The woman disappeared back around the corner.

"Only if you promise to rest later," Labren immediately

demanded. He caught her hand as she moved to rise. Cradling her face with his other palm, he stroked her cheek with his thumb. "I want you to take care of yourself. Ireic, Han, and Olof all back me up when I say you do not take care of yourself enough."

Eve hated the way the lines deepened around his mouth when he worried. It had been an almost constant feature over these last months.

"I will rest after she leaves." She placed her free hand over his and pressed it hard against her cheek. "I promise."

A half hour later, the women and Isica retired to the gardens.

"Trahern seemed extra agitated this morning," Yulandra observed as she and Eve watched Isica running after a butterfly. "Is something wrong between you two?"

They were sitting on the patio adjacent Eve and Labren's living area. Eve loved this part of the gardens. All the green and space were wonderful to see after the coldness of the palace halls and the strict paces of the dance. The warm spring afternoon sun played with the shadows across the lawn and a gentle breeze ruffled Isica's hair.

Eve looked over at her new friend.

Yulandra looked and acted like a princess. Her clothing displayed riches and beauty without being gaudy. She could gracefully glide across a room without thinking about the curve of her slender neck or where her hands should lay. Although obviously Ireic's sister and Labren's half-sister, she was also clearly feminine. Even now as she bent her dark head over the white linen in her hands, she defined composure and elegance. Her slender hands with their long, tapered fingers were constantly making something. Eve, who had sewn all her life, still wondered at the beauty of the embroidery that Yulandra could produce with her needle and colored thread.

"Eve? Are you listening to me at all?" Yulandra's dark brown eyes regarded her with mild concern.

"I am sorry." Quickly, Eve picked up her forgotten fabric and resumed basting the seam. "I have been so easily distracted lately. What was your question again?"

"Is there anything wrong between you and Trahern? He seemed a bit out of sorts this morning."

Eve felt a slight blush creep across her cheeks. "No, there is nothing wrong."

"Then why are you blushing?" Leaning forward, Yulandra raised Eve's chin. "Tell me about it. I might be able to help, being an experienced wife and all."

They both smiled at the statement. Yulandra had been married all of three months in which she only saw her husband for one week. That one week had given her Isica, for whom, Yulandra told Eve, she was inexpressibly grateful. The child was the reason she survived the death of her husband and, shortly afterwards, her mother.

"I have been having trouble for a week now with an upset stomach," Eve finally admitted.

"About what time of day?" Her sister-in-law immediately asked with widened eyes.

"Mornings." Puzzled at the woman's response, Eve tilted her head. "He only found out about it this morning because he did not leave as early as usual."

"Tell me more." The woman set aside her stitching and gave Eve her full attention.

"It started a week ago." Eve tried to think of anything else that could be important. "Every morning I wake up with the need to empty my stomach. After I do, I am fine." Looking at her friend's focused features, Eve started to feel a little worried.

"Have you had any trouble with dizziness or wanting certain foods?" Yulandra counted the items off on her slim fingers as Eve nodded at each. Yulandra smiled brightly and jumped to her feet. "I know what is wrong with you." Eve looked at her in amazement.

"You are happy about this?" Hesitant to believe what she saw, Eve glanced around for Isica.

"Eve." Yulandra caught her hands and pulled her to her feet. "You are pregnant."

Eve felt faint. Sitting abruptly, she gripped the arms of the chair.

"Eve?" Yulandra knelt at her feet. Eve fought the waves of emotion. "Do you want me to get you something? I have never seen you look so pale."

Eve shook her head before managing, "H . . . how do I tell Trahern?"

"Whatever do you mean?" This time Yulandra looked

confused. "This is the best news a wife can give her husband."

"It is?"

"Of course. A child, a son, an heir . . . Eve, every man wants children, especially Trahern."

Isica, who had been trying to catch a grasshopper near the edge of the rosebushes, suddenly jumped up and ran out of sight with a cry. "T'en! I'ic!"

Eve felt even sicker. Her connection to the world suddenly wobbled and her stomach tied in a knot.

Yulandra leaned close. "If you want, I will tell him."

Eve shook her head as Ireic and Labren appeared from behind the roses. Han was with them and surprisingly, he was the one carrying Isica. Noticing this, Yulandra lost a little of her own composure.

"Ah, girls," Ireic smiled as they approached.

Immediately noting Eve's coloring, Labren moved quickly to her side. While the others exchanged greetings behind them, he leaned close.

"Why are you out here? You promised me you would rest."

His dark blue eyes were even darker than usual.

Unfortunately for Labren, his gentle rebuke was the last straw and the emotions of the entire morning and afternoon suddenly seemed too much.

"Yulandra says I am pregnant." Eve fled inside.

Pregnant… their child… Slowly and carefully, Labren sat down in the chair Eve had just vacated. Eve was with child. For some crazy reason, he had forgotten about this possibility. It made sense, considering the changes in their relationship two and a half months before, but a child? A quiet joy began to grow in his chest.

"Trahern? Is Eve all right?"

Ireic's voice cut through his thoughts. Raising his eyes to focus on his brother's face, Labren realized the reason they had made this unusual trip to the garden was no longer possible.

"We cannot stay longer." Ireic's face took on an odd look of confusion and surprise.

"What do you mean you cannot stay? Stay here now or the proposal we discussed? Did you ask her?"

"No, but I have decided we are leaving as soon as we possibly can." Before his brother could manage the question on the tip of his tongue, Labren explained. "Eve is going to have a child." Pushing himself out of the chair, Labren turned and went in search of his wife.

Han and Ireic looked after him in a stunned silence. Finally Yulandra spoke. "I take it you were trying to persuade him to stay longer."

"Yes, and he seemed sold on the idea a moment ago," Han replied. He set the squirming Isica on the ground. She dove for the nearest grasshopper. Wondering what it would be like to be a father, he slowly turned back to the King and his sister. He was surprised to find Yulandra watching him with a look that he refused to analyze.

Oblivious to the silent exchange, Ireic sat down in a nearby chair. He ran his hands over his head, neatly avoiding the circle of gold among the strands. "I guess I am going to have to negotiate that marriage contract with the King of Sardmara after all."

Isica, with a crow of triumph, pounced upon a slow-moving moth only to have it evade her at the last moment.

"Eve?" Labren pushed aside the door so he could see into the bedroom. His wife was nowhere in sight. He opened his mouth to call again when a soft sound drew his attention to the floor on the opposite side of the bed. With quick strides, he crossed the room and rounded the end.

His wife sat with her back to the wall. As he approached, she raised her face. Tear trails traced over her cheeks. She flashed him a wobbly smile.

"Sorry I left."

Labren settled in front of her with his back against their bed before he spoke.

"Why are you crying?"

When she did not reply, he looked up and met her watery gaze. Her bottom lip trembled and he could not stand the distance any more. Reaching over, he pulled her into his lap. Silently, she curled against him.

After a few moments during which he stroked her hair, she finally said, "I was frightened that you would be angry."

"Sweetheart!" Labren tried to get her to look up, but she only burrowed deeper against him. "Please let me see your face,

Eve," he pleaded.

Reluctantly, she raised her head, but still would not look at his eyes. She concentrated on his chin.

"I love you." His voice sounded rougher than he had intended. "And I am going to love our child."

Finally, Eve lifted her eyes to his.

"Thank you," she whispered.

"No, I should be the one saying thank you." Labren caught her precious face between his hands. "Because Kurios brought you to me I am alive and going to be a father." After kissing her damp cheeks, he drew back and smiled. "If you had not been stubborn about not letting me die, I would have never reconciled with my brother or sister. Isica would have never have known her Uncle T'en and I would have never had the joy of loving you.

"Beloved, a child is the most wonderful gift you could ever give me." Unable to find the words to express all he felt, Labren possessively tucked his wife close to his heart. He planned on spending the rest of his life savoring her sweetness and making her happy.

Muffled against his chest, Eve whispered, "I love you too."

Epilogue

"They are here!" Three young boys tore through the front door and into the hall. The sound of their progress bounced off the ceiling two stories up. Between their repeated cries and the pounding of their feet, Eve heard them long before they skidded to a stop outside the doors leading to the back balcony.

"Ireic...came!" Turic gasped.

"Yulandra too." A Ratharian lad named Randare danced with excitement.

"Boys." Eve began the slow process of easing her way out of the chair. "Remember your manners." Timoty caught her falling needlework as she rose and what little lap she had disappeared. "He is the king of Anavrea. I will be sadly disappointed if you do not show him the proper respect."

Just because she was not longer teaching, Eve did not see it as an excuse for the children to run wild.

"We will, Madam Theodoric. We promise." Turic reassured her as she followed them toward the stairs. Timoty scurried ahead of them to let the new arrivals know she was coming. Eve watched enviously as he slid around the corner and clopped down the stairs.

"If only I could do that again."

Ruefully she glanced down at her blossoming stomach. Considering her small size and the fact the baby was due any day, Eve reasoned she was probably a healthy size. Regardless of these important facts, she could not help feeling awkward, heavy, and big as a boat.

"Ouch." The child followed up his first jab with another. "You know." Eve rubbed the top of her stomach. "I will not miss you kicking, little one. I am surprised I am not bruised from your abuse."

"Are you talking to the child again?" Labren's voice interrupted her one-sided conversation.

"Our little one is anxious to be free." Eve greeted her

husband with a smile. He appeared so much better than when they were in Ana City, the worry lines around his mouth softened and the tension gone from his movements.

"Soon," Labren replied as he pulled her against his side and spread his large hand over hers. After a brief silence between the three of them, Isica's glad cry came wafting up to them from the hall below.

Eve laughed.

"I think your niece has discovered her new playmates."

"Our niece," Labren reminded her. "Poor Yulandra."

"Why is it 'Poor Yulandra'?"

"The children are going to spoil Isica rotten."

"Then let us go rescue the poor woman." Eve put herself in motion once again. "Besides, I have a million mother questions for her."

Labren quickly moved to regain his place at her side. Offering her his arm, he asked, "Shall we go and be good hosts?"

Placing her hand on the offered support, Eve flashed him a brilliant smile. "Lead the way, my love."

About the Author

As a mother of three small children, Rachel Rossano dreams of new stories among the chaos of diapers and sippy cups. Then she writes as fast as she can during naptimes and after the little ones are tucked in for the night. She draws from a long history as an avid reader and lover of books. Usually she writes fantasy novels that masquerade as historical, but she recently spent time in the science and speculative fiction genres.

Come and visit her at:

http://rachel-rossano.blogspot.com
http://anavrea.webs.com

Also by Rachel Rossano

The Mercenary's Marriage

Exchange

The King of Anavrea

by Rachel Rossano

Ireic Theodoric, King of Anavrea, needed a wife. His kingdom required heirs. Unwilling to entertain the possibility of love, Ireic sought a quick decision, a political alliance.

For five years, Lady Lirth Parnan prayed her father would send a champion. Ireic offered the hope of freedom, a life beyond her tower prison. Could she hope for his love as well?

The King of Anavrea

The stone walls of the tower cooled her hands in spite of the unseasonable warmth of the past week. Gratefully, Lirth leaned her forehead against the rough stone. The cold surface chilled her fevered skin.

The distant clash of metal against metal echoed in the corridor and stairwell outside the thick oak door of her room. The din grew closer and she grasped at the calm she had felt only moments before.

I realized this day would come, yet... She caught herself mid thought. She should be thankful that she could prepare. Frustration flared and she asked, *Why must patience be so difficult?*

The unseen Kurios did not respond. He was there and she knew He was the source of her intuition.

It is not that I am not thankful. She pointed out. *Your intervention is the sole reason I have not been more battered. Instead of abusing me or using me, they isolate me.*

After her abduction five summers before, Baron Tor locked Lirth away in the cold tower room and forbade his men from speaking to her. By the grace of the Kurios, he chose not to execute her or hand her over to one of his minions. She had opportunity to cherish the hope of freedom.

The clanging below ceased. A death cry echoed within the stone tower below her prison.

Realizing the sound indicated someone would be seeking her soon, she paced the distance from the wall to her cot on the opposite side of the room. Her heavy cloak caught on the corner of the single chair as she passed. She wrenched it free.

Outside the door the wooden stairs creaked and groaned. The victor climbed to claim his prize.

Lirth's hands shook. She missed when she reached for her satchel. The second swipe caught the band for strapping it to her waist. She moved back toward the chair in the center of the room, tying the leather as she walked.

The wooden bolt struck the floor outside with a clatter.

Her fingers traced the worn lip along the back of the chair, seeking the familiar scratches. She measured her breaths by a two count to keep from panic.

The door uttered a grating squeal. The dull thud of wood striking the wall and rebounding reverberated in the bare room.

I hope it hit him.

She drew back the thought. The Kurios would not send someone to harm her.

What about those that sent him?

Nothing.

"Please tell Lady Lirth I have come for her." A warm male voice spoke above her head and about four feet in front of her.

"I am the one you seek."

Raising her chin so she addressed his face, Lirth drew herself up.

"Am I allowed to know the name of the one who seeks me?"

The slight change in the man's breathing warned Lirth of the man's astonishment before he spoke.

"They did not tell you?" Surprise lingered in his question, along with a hint of uncertainty.

"I was told nothing."

She heard his movement only a moment before he touched her.

"What is your full name?" Warm fingers caught her chin and gently forced her to turn. Flinching at the rough material of his gloves, Lirth closed her eyes and obeyed the man's verbal and physical commands.

"Lirth Yra Parnan, only daughter of Tridan, King of Sardmara."

Silence descended between them. The strange man studied her. His grip on her chin was gentle, but firm when she pushed against his fingers. After she tried to move away a second time, she gave up. Waiting, she reached out with her senses to examine him in return.

He smelled of battle: blood, sweat, and dirt. Beneath these, though, she detected a waft of the soap he bathed with recently. His hands were long and lean. Although he held her face firmly, she doubted she would be tender or bruised later.

Concentrating on their brief exchange, she guessed him to be about six feet tall, maybe slightly over. He must be fit, because his breathing though accelerated was not rushed. Four flights of stairs stretched from the tower's base to the room.

Unfortunately she could not guess at his age or features. She needed her own fingers and his permission for that.

When he finally spoke, his voice sounded calmer and quieter, tone controlled.

"Ireic Iathan Theodoric, King of Anavrea." He paused. "Open your eyes, Lirth, and look at me."

"I cannot obey you."

Steeling herself for a blow, Lirth was stunned when he spoke instead.

"Why not?"

She opened her eyes to the darkness she had known most of her life.

"I am blind."

Coming Soon

BOOK TWO – THE THEODORIC SAGA

The King of Anavrea

by Rachel Rossano

EXCHANGE

A SHORT STORY

by Rachel Rossano

He offers her escape...

Isolated on a distant planet, she is incarcerated for a crime she doesn't recall. She has no name, no idea where she came from, or why she is injected with drugs to hold these vital facts from her grasp. Despite small rebellions, she wastes away, worn and losing hope of ever being whole again. Then he arrives. Claiming to hold the answers burned daily from her brain, he offers her a way out.

...but at what cost?

EXCHANGE -

Darkness enveloped me completely. I breathed stuffy blackness in labored pants, struggling to tolerate the closeness. Cottony, the warmth threatened to suffocate me in a billowing blanket of malevolence.

I hated when I woke early.

The sensors glued to my forehead and scalp screamed to be scratched, but the arm bands made that impossible. I mentally clawed for something to fixate on, anything other than the inching six walls trapping me.

Why they called the box a dream suite I don't know. I never dreamed and it only barely contained me. Six by three by two feet, it was built to contain one average sized human. One of thirty stacked like drawers in one wall of the ward. I supposed I should have been thankful that I was a below-average-sized humanoid. Sometimes I managed to ignore the walls because I wasn't constantly in contact with them, only the padded pseudo-bed beneath my back. However, no matter how I strained, I couldn't truly believe they didn't exist.

With a soft hiss, jets of cold air bombarded my naked feet signaling the waking time. The weight on my chest dissipated slightly in the cooler air, but in its place nagged the raw instinct to tuck my freezing feet closer to my body. I couldn't bend my legs far enough. The knowledge degenerated into panic. Hysteria edged in just as a hum and jolt warned me to check that my eyes stayed closed.

Another whirling hum, jolt, and sucking whoosh later, piercing blue light assaulted my face as my chamber drew out of the wall into the ward. Arm restraints retracted into the sides.

"Down, female, 7682R."

The droid's grating mechanical voice invaded the borders of my mind, setting my teeth hard against each other. A final blast of icy air from the suite's jets meant to encourage me to move faster did the exact opposite.

The rebel in me itched to defy the automaton until a humanoid showed her face. However, the penalty wasn't worth the temporary high of asserting my own will. My skin crawled at the memory of the waspmice. Dark pock-like scars still marred my legs from last time. I clamored out of the DS and padded barefoot across the slick floor to the cleansing stations on the far side of the room.

The android, a bulky P-73, stalked behind, whining through its exhaust hose. It probably worried I would throw another fit or fall into hysterics. I was allowed to remember a few bits from day to day, like incidents of rebellion and punishments. With drugs and therapy, they attempted to erase the rest.

My skin crawled. I concentrated on unlatching the sealed door on the cleanser and climbing inside the chamber. A deep breath to brace myself and I pulled the panel closed. Alternating jets of tepid and steaming water blasted me from all angles. I ripped the rubber suction cells off my skin and threw them in the refuse slot. My temples throbbed where the probes had recently entered my skull. A light touch of my fingertips brought away blood. I wondered how many times had I stood here. I didn't know. It was disconcerting to never remember one day to the next.

A pathetic sputter of water-flecked air constituted the cleanser's attempt at drying my abused skin before a panel popped open with a belch of perfumed air. I coughed as I reached for the two-piece jumpsuit contained within. My arms executed the complicated movements of dressing myself without much direction from my thoughts. I knew I had been here long enough for this routine to become rote, unless, of course, I had worn clothing just like this before I came here. Or maybe I had always been here?

EXCHANGE

A SHORT STORY

by Rachel Rossano

Available Now

Smashwords
http://www.smashwords.com/books/view/92034

and

Amazon Kindle
http://www.amazon.com/Exchange-ebook/dp/B005PTXWDI

Made in the USA
Las Vegas, NV
08 January 2024

84092895R00073